For Samuel Lee, Marieka Mee Sung, and Lucas Choi

STRINGZ

Michael Wenberg

WestSide Books
Lodi, New Jersey

Published by WestSide Books
60 Industrial Road
Lodi, NJ 07644
973-458-0485
Fax: 973-458-5289

Library of Congress Cataloging-in-Publication Data

Wenberg, Michael.
  Stringz / by Michael Wenberg. -- 1st ed.
      p. cm.
  Summary: Fourteen-year-old Jace Adams, a cellist who loves to
surf,
never fits in where his mother decides to move them, but after a
difficult start in Seattle, he comes to realize that talent is not
something to hide and that he has "family" in some unexpected
places.
  ISBN 978-1-934813-33-1
  [1. Interpersonal relations--Fiction. 2. Moving, Household--Fiction. 3.
Cellists--Fiction. 4. High schools--Fiction. 5. Schools--Fiction. 6.
Racially mixed people--Fiction. 7. Family life--Washington
(State)--Fiction. 8. Seattle (Wash.)--Fiction.] I. Title.
  PZ7.W4689Str 2010
  [Fic]--dc22

                                                            2010009040

International Standard Book Number: 978-1-934813-33-1
School ISBN: 978-1-934813-35-5
Cover design by David Lemanowicz
Interior design by David Lemanowicz

Printed in the United States of America
10 9 8 7 6 5 4 3 2 1

First Edition

1

Freshman year sucks.

If you're a freshman like me, you know what I'm talking about. If you're still stuck in junior high or middle school, you probably think I'm crazy. But just wait—you'll see. And if you're lucky enough to already be a sophomore or junior, well, just think back. . . . Oh yeah, you *know* I'm right.

Like I said, freshman year sucks.

Okay, okay, I know I have a bad attitude. But so what? I'm entitled. That's because I happen to be working on my fourth new school in less than two years. How would *you* like it?

In fact, it's been so crazy the past couple of years I've barely had enough time to figure out the location of the safe bathrooms at a school before Mom hauls me off to somewhere new—again. But she always has a very good reason: better job, shorter commute, more money, nicer apartment, blah, blah, blah. . . . She even promised that this was going to be our last move—because she finally had a *really* good job.

Yeah, right. Whatever. That's what she said last time. I didn't bother to point it out to her, though. I wasn't in the mood to get smacked—again.

But this time was supposed to be different—because we'd be living with Aunt Bernice. That meant we didn't have to worry about finding a cheap place to stay, only to move again when the neighborhood turned out to be a war zone. Or because the gross and hairy building manager decided to get a little too interested in my mom. Ugh. Anyway, you can't blame me for not expecting us to stay put this time, Aunt Bernice or not. I figured it was just a matter of time before we'd be packing up and on the move again.

Even so, on my way to school that first morning, I was momentarily fooled into thinking that this year might turn out to be okay—that maybe, just maybe, this move might stick for a change.

And it didn't hurt that I could actually see the sun—that was a surprise! Everybody knows Seattle's rep: it's rain, rain, and then more rain. And when it isn't raining, the sky is a solid sheet of gray and it's getting ready to rain. That's how it had been since we'd arrived in the middle of the night a couple of days before. I figured all those pictures of a sunny Seattle had to be Photoshopped. I guess it was nice to be wrong and find out that the sun did actually come out once in a while.

As I walked towards the high school that day, I didn't think I'd ever seen a sky so blue. The air smelled clean and fresh, and even the trees and grass seemed greener. And I wasn't even bugged that—thanks to Mom being completely, well, Mom—we'd left L.A. later than we planned, meaning that the school year had already started a few weeks earlier—without me.

Not that starting later really made much difference to me. I was used to parachuting into new schools just about any time of the year. But here's the deal: for the first time in what seemed like forever, I was actually feeling—there was only one word for it—*good*.

Don't get me wrong. I didn't think it would last. I'm not that dumb. But I also wasn't dumb enough to wreck it. I mean, it's like in surfing: when you're feeling good, you *ride* that wave as long as you can. Because you know that soon enough, you're gonna wipe out. And when you do, you just get back on your board, paddle out beyond the break, and wait for another set of waves. That's one of the reasons I liked surfing: there's always another chance.

Yeah, that's right. I used to be a surfer. But before we left L.A., Mom made me get rid of my board.

"What are you going to do with a surfboard in Seattle?" she said, talking to me like I was a complete idiot. Well, maybe I am an idiot. The nearest waves were . . . who knows where? I had no idea, even if I could scare up another board. A normal mom would've realized how much her kid was into surfing and maybe considered that before picking a new place to live.

But my mom wasn't exactly what you'd call normal—never was, either. What she did have was what I called a bad case of "the opposites." If you told her to stop, she'd give you a look and keep going. If you said to turn left, she'd turn right instead. And if you said, "No way, no how are you ever going to be able to do that," she'd just stick out her chin and try even harder, just to prove you wrong.

I hadn't said anything to her about it yet, but as soon as I was old enough, I was gone. Back to L.A. or maybe San Diego. Or better yet, maybe even farther south, like Mexico, or perhaps way west to Hawaii or even Tahiti. I've always heard that Tahiti has killer surf. I've heard the girls are killer, too.

So I used to keep in touch with a girl from two or three schools ago. She's in Phoenix now, I think. Her name is Kari. Before Mom took away my cell phone, we'd text each other and keep in touch. Anyway, when we used to talk, every once in a while, she used a phrase that's stuck with me ever since. She'd say, "It is what it is."

Here's how it looked when she'd send me a text: IIWII.

So now, whenever I think about those words, it makes me, like, feel better. Simple as that. It's the same as when I'm eating a hamburger that tastes like crap; I just think, *It is what it is*. It doesn't make that burger taste any better, but it just doesn't matter as much to me. And when I start getting twisted about something Mom's done (or hasn't done), I just think, *It is what it is*, and then it doesn't bug me the way it did.

And so for me, that first day of school in Seattle, I was even ready to believe that for once in my life, anything could be possible. While I didn't expect to see ten-footers pounding a Seattle beach any time soon, maybe I really would move back to California someday. And maybe I'd discover that the pawnshop still had my surfboard—and it'd be on sale, cheap. And I'd get straight A's. And I'd find out before we took off again that the hottest girl in school thought I was hot, too—and that she was moving to California and we'd be going to the same high school. . . .

Even if you're a loser, the first time you walk into a new school, you can still fool yourself into thinking that maybe you're really not so bad and that things will turn out okay. What I didn't know was that this fantasy would only last, like, thirty seconds—just about as long as it'd take me to hop out of Mom's car, run up the steps to the landing, and then stroll into the school like I owned the place.

2

First of all, I want to make it perfectly clear that what happened next wasn't my fault—not really.

I had to admit that at first glance, Ben Franklin High School wasn't the hellhole I'd expected. No graffiti on the walls, no pee stink in the hallways; everything was clean and neat, and it smelled like fresh floor polish. There was the usual rush as students headed for their first-period classes. And after being back to school for three weeks already, they all knew where they were going. I was a newbie, but nobody gave me a second look, even though I was carrying a big old cello case.

Yeah, I play the cello. If you're not familiar with it, imagine an overgrown violin—that's what a cello looks like. It's too big to tuck under your chin like a violin, so you have to play it sitting down, holding it between your knees. It has a big spike at the bottom to keep it from sitting on the ground. Most of the guys I know don't even play musical instruments. They're into video games or sports— or just hanging out. So no matter where I am, me and the cello kinda stick out.

Maybe if I'd had a choice, I'd have picked something else to play—something cool but less noticeable. But I was only six when Mom got me my first cello and made me start to learn it. See, she had a crush on this famous cellist—the great one with what sounded to me like a made-up name: Yo-Yo Ma. I'm serious—that's really his name. Yeah, she thought this guy was so cool; she had all his CDs. Coulda been worse; at least she didn't change my name to Yo-Yo.

Since I've been playing cello, I've had three of them. My favorite's the one I have now. I call her Ruby because the wood's stained kind of reddish. The ruby's also my birthstone. Maybe it's just a coincidence, but I don't think so.

Anyway, as I walked down the hall that first day, I thought, *So far, so good.* I took a deep breath and started to relax. Big mistake! That's because as I walked, I noticed a knot of kids gathering on the other side of the foyer. And inside that knot, I could see three big guys picking on a tall, skinny kid, a kid made even taller by his fountain of bright red, curly hair.

What a complete idiot. Everyone knows the first rule of surviving at any high school: make sure you don't do anything to stand out or get noticed. Tall and skinny was bad enough, but having red hair standing up like that was the same as having a tat on your forehead saying, "PLEASE KICK THE CRAP OUT OF ME."

Everyone also knows you can only ignore this rule if you happen to be protected by your own posse of like-minded idiots. Having a few friends with you is a good thing, unless the guys you're going up against have chains or bats or semi-automatic weapons. When that happens, you do whatever they want you to do, no questions asked—or else you run really fast.

I looked around, but no gang of tall, skinny red-headed kids suddenly appeared. Which leads me to my second rule of surviving a new school: when the shit starts to hit the fan, you gotta keep moving and think like a shark. If you quit moving, you can die—or at least run into serious trouble. So above all, keep going until you're in the clear—or at least safely in your seat in class.

But that day, for whatever reason, I decided to ignore rule number two. Dumb, I know. But it was an easy mistake to make, since I was feeling so good. So I stopped and watched as they grabbed Skinny Kid and flipped him upside down, dumping the contents of his backpack on the floor.

Okay, jerks. You've had your fun. Leave him alone. But I knew that even if I said something out loud, it wouldn't make any difference. They were like any other carnivores that were near the top of the food chain—a wolf pack tormenting a caribou or tigers chasing a wildebeest. Okay, I admit it; I probably watch too much Animal Planet.

As I checked them out, these three looked so much alike, they could have been clones: they all had scraggly beards that didn't quite cover up their zits; they all dressed in faded jeans, and their tight gray T-shirts showed off every muscle. Man, they didn't have six-packs; they had ten-packs. Now, I'm no expert, but either they all got lucky in the gene pool crapshoot or they all brushed with steroid-flavored toothpaste—assuming they even brushed. There was just no way these three high school guys could have that much muscle without serious chemical help—I don't care how many hours they spent lifting in the gym.

Anyway, instead of killing Skinny Kid and tearing into his still-twitching carcass, they dropped him on his head and swept all of his stuff into a pile—using his face for a broom. They were all laughing like they'd just discovered a new game.

I know—it doesn't make sense to have rules unless you plan to follow them. So no excuses—I still had a choice and could have kept moving. I mean, it wasn't like this poor kid meant anything to me. I was just starting out in a new school. Why wreck it on my first day? In the past few years, I'd learned that staying off the radar was a great way to survive, and right now, I was still about as invisible as I would ever be here—at least as much as I could be, lugging around this big freakin' cello case.

So I shifted the cello case to my other hand and looked around, expecting to see a teacher or maybe a security guard. But there was nobody. What the hell was going on? At my other schools, there was always some sort of adult, cop, teacher, or whatever—or at least a camera keeping an eye on things. No way could this stuff happen without somebody noticing. But it looked like nobody was going to show up in time to help this kid.

With nobody in charge, I still had time to get out of there, and I could feel the impulse to run tugging at me. But for some reason, I stayed put. Maybe I'm just a freak or something—no different from people who watch something bad happening but are too chicken or enjoying it too much to try and stop it. Since I wasn't a chicken, I guess it meant it was kinda fun watching the zit-faced trio use Skinny Kid like a push broom.

But then they started tugging at the case he'd managed to hang onto with a death grip the whole time. If he'd just dropped it, they wouldn't have even noticed it. But since he clung to it like he was desperate, they figured it had to be worth grabbing. Plus, Skinny Kid made these pathetic little squeals with every tug. That pitiful sound just egged them on.

I wanted to yell at him to shut up—not that it would've done any good. And it'd get me on their radar—and I didn't want to go there. So I shut up and watched as the jerk in charge looked around, then kidney-punched Skinny Kid. *Ouch. That had to hurt.* And it did the trick. Skinny Kid let go of his case, and they forgot about him. *The poor dork.* He may have been asking for it, but thanks to Oprah, I'm not a totally insensitive jerk. I'd learned most of what I knew about right, wrong, and injustice from Oprah. If she'd been around to see this, she'd have waded in on these guys and kicked some serious bully ass. But I guess, being that she's just about the richest woman in the world, she wouldn't do it herself. She'd have *her people* wade in and kick some serious bully ass. All it would take would be a little wave of her hand and it'd be all over. Where was Oprah when you really needed her?

As I was considering Oprah's place in the world of injustice, I noticed Skinny Kid was finally doing something right: he'd curled up in a ball on the floor, covering his face and head with his arms. I watched the bully-in-chief step away from his two sidekicks and push through the crowd. As he turned in my direction, he flipped open the case and pulled out the most beautiful violin I'd ever seen. But instead of treating it with the respect it deserved, he grabbed it by the neck, raised it over his head, let out a scream, and waved it around like it was some kind of caveman club.

That's when something went *click* inside my head. What'd this asshole think he was doing? If he wasn't careful, he'd damage that righteous musical instrument—and I wasn't gonna let that happen. When I was a little kid, my older brother, Derrick, taught me that you *always* respect musical instruments. I hadn't thought about it much—until that fool started waving that violin around. Now I had to do something. Since Oprah wasn't going to magically appear on the scene and make everyone play nice, and since Derrick, well, he wasn't around, either, that left it to me; they'd forced my hand. *Ah, crap.* So much for staying off the radar and that wave of good first-day feelings.

I set down my cello, put my glasses in my battered backpack, and tossed it into the corner. *This is about the stupidest thing you've ever done,* I told myself. *But you can still stop.* I even hesitated for a second before lunging ahead and yelling, "Come on, man. You don't wanna do that. Just put down the violin."

I sounded like a moron. Seriously, I could have come up with something better, like "Yo, dude, chill with that violin." But at the sound of my words, the bully with the violin froze. And then he spotted me, and a smirk formed on his ugly face, as if he couldn't believe someone who looked like me could be so lame. I'm not exactly what you'd call *buff.* On a good day, someone could call me wiry. There's a scar on my chin, but only from getting hit by my own surfboard. Nothing in my genes from my African-American mom and my white Irish dad—who I didn't even know— was going to help me right now. So it wasn't like I was surprised when he sneered, "What'd you say, asshole?"

That's when I remembered my secret weapon. Derrick used to call them "a black man's brass knuckles." *Damn right.* I grabbed the roll of quarters I'd almost left back at Aunt Bernice's. And as I waited for the bully to take a swing at me, I noticed Skinny Kid getting to his feet. But all he did was just stand there and gape at me. *Jackass!* I felt a sudden flush of anger; if he wasn't such a chicken shit, he could help me out. I mean, it was *his* violin I was trying to save. But even as I was calling him a jackass in my head, I knew that the real fool here was me. I was the one who should have kept walking. I was the one who had to go and open his big mouth. *What was I thinking?* But it was way too late to change my mind.

Then, in a flash, I realized that if I was lucky and if Skinny Kid was less of an idiot than I figured, maybe I could still save his violin. But if my stunt didn't work, the violin could still get wrecked and this whole episode would end in bloodshed—mine. That's when the bully decided to do something stupid even for him: he got right up in my face, holding onto the violin like he was going to brain me with it instead of smacking it against the wall.

"So what's up, tough guy?" he said. "You gonna get in my face? I'm about to seriously mess you up. Maybe I'll rip off your head and stuff this little guitar down your throat. I destroy wusses like you for breakfast."

"Guess what, dude," I interrupted, proud that my voice wasn't shaking.

"Wha'?" said the tough guy, the smirk back on his face.

"It's a *violin*," I said.

He wrinkled his brow, like I was speaking Swahili.

"It's a violin, you big jerk," I said with contempt, "not a guitar." I saw his pupils dilate, and I knew I had maybe a nanosecond before he broke the violin over my head. In one motion, I took a quick step forward and nailed him under the ribs with the roll of quarters.

He let out a gasp and doubled over, gasping for breath. While he was still dazed, I could've grabbed him by the back of the head and busted his nose on my knee. But I still had that violin to worry about. So instead of finishing him off, I wrenched the violin from him and flipped it in the direction of Skinny Kid. Yeah—that was my big plan. I just hoped he was still there and wouldn't fumble the catch.

Then, somebody screamed—and before I could hit the moron again, I got tackled from behind at about the same time as the roll of quarters came apart in my hand, sending ten dollars in change flying all over the hallway. To a teenager, a hailstorm of quarters isn't something you ignore, and all the kids who'd been spectators of this little ass-kicking episode were now shrieking and chasing the coins that rolled in every direction.

As I lay there, sprawled on the floor, an adult finally skidded around the corner. *About time*. The last thing I heard was "Hey—you boys there—stop!"

And then I got smacked in the head and it was lights out.

3

They dumped me on a cot in the school nurse's office. It was like other nurse's offices I'd seen—the same drab cabinets for bandages and aspirin, the barf-proof walls, and the boring health posters with slogans about how bullies are bad, how guns are bad, too (especially if you bring them to school), how drugs are bad, and how there's no such thing as safe sex. *Blah, blah, blah.* I was still woozy and had no idea who'd brought me there. I just remember being carried and then tumbling onto the bed. And they left me hanging there, not even bothering to put my legs up with the rest of me.

I closed my eyes, and I heard someone come into the room to put something cold in my hand and then leave again—without saying a word. I guess they figured I'd know to stick that ice pack on my forehead. It felt great, and I pulled my legs up onto the mattress with a sigh. I didn't know what was going to happen next, but this wasn't half bad. Even though classes were going on, here I was on a bed, relaxing with an ice bag on my head. It was probably still sunny outside, and if I was lucky, my face was so banged up and bruised that nobody'd recognize me once the swelling went down. Then I could go back to being invisible. *Sweet.*

I lay there for five minutes or so, nodding off, then was startled awake at the sound of someone yelling from down the hall. I hoped it meant one of those bullies was now catching the crap they deserved. As I listened to the continuing noise, I realized it'd soon be my turn to get grilled by some principal. And I wasn't proud; I'd howl, too, if it helped get me out of trouble. I figured I'd get suspended for a day or two, minimum. Or at least get a warning stuck in my file. Great way to start off at a new school—with a black mark on my permanent record. I'd also have to deal with whatever my mom would do to me. Oh, yeah. *That'll be fun.*

Worst case, I could always play the missing daddy card and blame it on the fact that my dad took off before I was even born. He just left Mom with Derrick in first grade and me in the oven. He never even bothered to send Mom any money, never wrote us a single letter, postcard, or birthday card—nothing. I had no idea where he was—or if he was even still alive. I was just another deprived teenager with serious anger-management issues. None of this was my fault—and that's how I'd play it. The daddy card hadn't failed me yet at school, but it wouldn't work with my mom.

At least I didn't have any history at this school—yet. And my records from the previous school probably hadn't caught up with me—yet. So maybe instead of kicking me out or calling my mom, someone'd come in and see if I was okay. Who knows? Maybe they'd even say I'd done a good thing, standing up for Skinny Kid and that violin.

4

Who was I kidding? Nobody came to check on me. And after lying in the nurse's office for a while, I tossed the bag of ice on the floor—it was mostly melted anyway—and I just lay there, tensing various muscles, feeling the ache in my stomach and the back of my head. I felt the inside of my mouth with my tongue—no broken teeth. *Whew.* I wiggled my toes and fingers, then checked my face; everything seemed to work—not that I was all that worried. I think I even slept a bit, then woke to the sound of someone clearing their throat. I kept my eyes closed, hoping they'd go away, but no such luck.

"I see you're awake." It was a pleasant, mom-sounding voice with just a hint of concern and kindness.

"Excuse me?"

"I said, 'I see you're awake.' "

"You must be the nurse."

"Last time I checked," she said. "My name is Mrs. Allen."

"What are you going to do with me?"

She thought a moment. "That depends. Anyone at home?"

I shook my head, trying not to wince.

"How do you feel? You can't be too careful with these kinds of injuries."

"You mean getting kicked in the head?" I said.

"Well, I was going to call it being foolish, but you probably already know all about that." She didn't hide her sarcasm.

"You got me there," I said.

"So what's your name?" she asked.

"Jace. Jace Adams," I stuttered.

"Jace? That's nice. Is it short for Jason?"

"It's short for nothin'," I said. "My mom heard the name Jace somewhere and always liked it. Lucky me."

"Well, Jace Adams, taking on three bullies was a pretty dumb thing to do. You should've gone for help instead. And I think you probably know that. But I admire your guts. Last time I checked, those three are about the toughest kids in school. *I'm* even a little afraid of them, and I used to be an ER nurse."

"Figures," I muttered to myself.

"What was that?" She cupped a hand behind her ear.

"I was just thinking," I said with a sigh, "I know how to pick 'em. Now they'll probably be hassling me all year. And when they're not making my life hell, they'll get their buddies to do it instead."

"I don't mean to puncture your balloon, but I'm sure they'll forget all about you by lunch," Mrs. Allen said.

Wanna bet? I'd embarrassed them, especially their

leader. *He'll remember me.* But I kept quiet. "You don't happen to know where my stuff is, do you?" I asked.

She motioned towards the door. "A friend of yours dropped them off."

"Friend?" I said, sitting up on one elbow. "I don't have any friends. Today's my first day; I'm new here."

"All freshmen are new here," she remarked.

"Well, sure," I replied, trying not to sound flustered. "But I'm *really* new. As in I just moved into town a few days ago."

"Okay, then. Let's just say that you're a bit fresher than the other freshmen. They've only had a three-week head start. Where you from?" She was now sitting on a stool by the counter, filling out a form attached to a clipboard.

"L.A."

"You must be glad to be in Seattle. This is a great place to live."

I squinted at her to make sure she wasn't kidding. She wasn't.

"Well, I don't know about a lack of friends," she said. "But you seem to have one now."

"How long have I been here?" I'd lost track of time and didn't see a clock.

"About forty minutes," she said, "give or take a few."

"Hey, what was going on with that screamer down the hall?"

"You mean Adrian?"

"Whatever. I guess so."

"I gave him some ibuprofen," she said, "then popped his dislocated finger back where it belonged—"

"How'd he dislocate his finger?" I wondered out loud. I was trying to remember if I'd managed to pull some sort of lucky ninja move on the bully—if that's who'd been yelling. I had no way of knowing if this Adrian was even one of them.

She put down her pencil, rapped her head with her knuckles, and then pointed at me. "Your hard head was the culprit," she said.

"Oh, crap," I said, wondering how I'd have to pay for that. Now not only did I stand up to those guys, I'd also managed to hurt one. I shook my head, then winced in pain.

The nurse noticed. "Try not to do that, Jace. You were hit in the back of the head."

Without thinking, I shook my head again, then immediately regretted it and moaned. "Not hit. Kicked, I think."

"That'll do it, too." She pushed away from the counter and handed me three pills and a glass of water. "Here, take these."

"What are they?" I asked.

"Ibuprofen. You'll thank me in about a half hour, when they start to work. I called your mom to get permission, but I only got her voice mail. Since you look like you need a painkiller, I'll take the heat if she objects. You aren't allergic to over-the-counter ibuprofen, are you?"

I caught myself before I shook my head again. "No," I said, tossing back the pills and gulping the water. I knew Mom wasn't going to be happy about any of this. Maybe this was how it'd all started with my brother: one day, he's in the nurse's office taking something for a headache; next thing, he's in jail at San Quentin for dealing.

"I'll be all right," I said. "Just give me a few minutes. No need to call my mom again, unless you think I'm going to be in some kind of trouble."

"Actually," she said, "I think you're free to go whenever you feel up to it."

"No way," I retorted.

"Absolutely," she insisted. "They said you could go as soon as you felt better. And if you don't feel better, I'll call your mom again and have her pick you up."

I'd figured I'd automatically be sent home. I'd been suspended from school before, but this would be a new record—suspended on my first day. But since that wasn't going to happen, maybe I could keep Mom out of it altogether; maybe today wasn't going to be a total loss after all.

"Before you go, you have to tell me one thing," she said quietly, pulling a chair close to my bed and peering over her shoulder.

"I will if I can," I said.

"Where'd you come up with the idea of the quarters?"

I gave her a blank look. "I don't know what you mean."

She rolled her eyes. "The roll of quarters! You most likely know that coming to school with brass knuckles will get you in big trouble; they're considered a weapon. But a roll of quarters? That's very clever. You can explain that away as just a boy's lunch money."

"Boy?" I said evenly.

She didn't back down. "Last time I checked, you were too young to drive or buy cigarettes, so yeah, *boy's* the proper word, regardless of your color."

"I'm still not sure what you mean," I said, all innocent and smiling.

"Right, I bet you don't," she said, more to herself than to me. "But I suspect I'll be seeing way too much of you this year—though I hope I'm wrong."

"You're wrong," I said. And I almost added that we'd be outta here in a few months anyway. But I kept quiet. The less anyone knew about me, the easier it'd be to stay invisible. Mrs. Allen smiled in a sad sort of way that made me think she knew something that I didn't.

"Maybe so, maybe not. But meanwhile, how do you feel now?"

"Okay." I was lying. My right hand hurt, and my head was sore. But I sensed an opening here. "I'm really all right," I insisted, giving her my unblinking, you-can-trust-me look.

"You don't have any of the obvious signs of a concussion," Mrs. Allen said, half to herself.

I could tell she was wavering, and it was time to push if I was going to get out of there. "If I starting feeling sick, I'll come back—I promise you."

She stood up and gestured towards the door, then handed me a hall pass. "Okay. Go to class. I have work to do."

"You mean, that's it?"

"That's it from me. You might hear from Mr. Ford, the vice principal."

"Ford like the car?" I asked.

"Ah, no. As in Mr. Ford, one very big, ornery vice principal."

She didn't need to explain. Vice principals couldn't afford to be nice. But I wasn't too worried; I hadn't met a Mr.

Ford yet that I couldn't handle. I stood up, wavered a little as all the blood in my body rushed towards my feet, and felt like throwing up; but I knew if I did, I'd be stuck there even longer.

"If you start getting sleepy, come see me."

"Yes, ma'am."

I grabbed my backpack, picked up my cello case, and slipped out. As I began trudging down the hall past the closed main office doors, I heard Mrs. Allen call out: "One more thing, Jace—"

I paused and leaned up against the wall for support. I felt pretty rotten. "Yeah?"

"Elvis wanted me to pass along his thanks."

"Elvis?"

"Your new friend—the kid you helped. He's the one who brought your backpack and cello. He told everyone what happened, and I think that's why Mr. Ford didn't need to see you—not yet, anyway."

Elvis? Skinny Kid even had a dork name. Figured. I checked the time on the hall clock; even with everything that'd happened, it was still the last part of first period. I pulled out my schedule, found the room number for my first class, and moved on. Then, something else occurred to me and I stopped. "Hey, Mrs. Allen."

She stuck her head out of the doorway again. "Yes?"

"Did he catch it?"

"Catch what?"

"The violin."

"Oh, my God," she gasped.

I frowned. "Why'd you say that? What happened?"

28

"You mean, you were actually tossing Elvis's violin around?" Her eyes narrowed.

"Well, those—dudes—grabbed it. And one of them, the dude I was, you know, trying to convince to give it back, well, he was waving it around like a bat. So I . . . um—"

"You what?" she asked sharply.

I chose my words carefully. "I, uh, was hoping that when I, uh, got it away from him and tossed it to—um—"

"Elvis," she offered.

"Right. Elvis. That Elvis would catch it. That was the plan, anyway."

"Plan?" Mrs. Allen grabbed the door frame. "So you worked this out with him ahead of time?"

"Not really."

"You either talked about it or not."

"I guess I just hoped he'd know to catch it. You know, like this *Star Wars* kinda mind reading thing," I said.

"Oh, so you used the Force," she mocked.

"Uh, yeah, sorta," I said, my heart sinking.

"Do you have any idea—no, of course not, there's no way you could know." She took a deep breath. "Let me just say that Elvis Goldberg is an accomplished violinist, maybe the best teenage violinist in the city or even in the whole Northwest. And that violin you tossed at him so casually was made in 1821 and is worth more than most people earn in year."

I gulped and suddenly felt my head spin a little. *Way to go, Jace.* "I knew that," I said. "So I guess he *really* owes me. It didn't look good for that violin, the way that bully was waving it around. What the heck was that kid—?"

29

"It's Elvis!" She almost shouted his name this time, and she looked like she wanted to strangle me.

"Whatever," I said. "I mean, what the heck was he doing, bringing such a valuable instrument to school, anyway? Showing off or something? I'm the one who should be upset. I got my ass kicked tryin' to save it."

Then I heard a door open into the hall behind me. "And you must be Mr. Adams," someone said in a quiet voice. I turned around and came face to face with a tall, bald black man. He was dressed in a black suit with a crisp white shirt and red tie, and he wore rimless eyeglasses that sparkled in the light. His face was a blank slate.

I pasted a smile on my face. "Hey, man," I said. "You got it. I'm Jace Adams. And you're . . . ?"

He nodded and smiled. "I'm Mr. Ford. One of the vice principals."

I thought for a brief moment and then stuck out my hand. What else could I do? "Howya doin', Mr. Ford?"

He glared at my hand, and then his features relaxed into a grin. "I have a feeling we're going to get to know each other well this year."

"No offense," I replied, "but I'm going to be outta here in a few months."

"We'll see," he said, with a knowing laugh. "Now, you'd better get to class before I change my mind and decide to let the police charge you with assault."

"Whaddya mean?" I asked, all innocent.

"Git out of here," he said, with just enough menace to make sure I didn't turn around and look back over my shoulder.

5

The rest of my day was mostly a blur. Maybe it was the kick in the head, hunger, or the whopping headache, but I don't really remember much after meeting Mr. Ford.

I caught up with my first-period class just before the bell rang, and then it was off to second period—English literature. I dozed through that class and woke up at the bell. Third period was chemistry and another nap. I did manage to rouse myself a couple of times when I caught myself drooling on my desk. That's when I noticed a girl on my right staring at me in complete disgust.

I spent lunch sitting on the curb in the parking lot, hungry and wishing I still had that roll of quarters so I could get a sandwich. After lunch, I headed to French class. Yeah, I know, French? Why not something useful like Chinese or Japanese or maybe even Spanish? But some great classical music was written by French composers like Ravel, and I thought it'd be good to check it out. And the great African-American singer Josephine Baker lived in France and sang some songs in French, too, and it'd be cool to understand the words. And they spoke French in Tahiti—a great place to surf. Whatever.

My final class of the day was orchestra—alright! I'd saved the best for last—or at least that's what I thought until I walked in there. The teacher was over six feet tall, but it was hard to tell because of the way he hunched over—almost as if he was trying to hide his height. He wore a tight white polo shirt with a little black horse on the chest, and his tight black pants were pulled up high enough that they probably raised his voice a whole octave.

"And who do we have here?" he asked, eyeing me as I stood in the doorway with my cello case. He checked me out from head to toe, then dismissed me with a wave. "Take a seat in the back, whoever you are—if you actually belong here."

His attitude set off warning bells inside my head—not a good thing, since it was still throbbing. No way did I deserve to be talked to that way—not by anyone—and he didn't even know me. Even though he was a teacher, I was half tempted to flip him off and head back to Bernice's. I could worry about the crap I'd get for it tomorrow. But I'd had enough trouble for one day; no sense looking for more. And this was, after all, orchestra class—the one place I actually *wanted* to be. So I forced a polite, friendly expression onto my face. "Yeah," I said, looking at my schedule. "This is where I'm supposed to be. Sorry if I'm late," I added, noticing that most of the kids were already in their seats and waiting to play.

He put one hand under his chin and gave me a closer look. "How long have you been playing the cello? Did you just pick it up today?"

I heard scattered laughter from the kids in the class, and my face burned. *Why me?* The way this orchestra teacher was treating me was no laughing matter. I checked my class schedule, just to make sure I had his name right: Mr. Whitehead. *Figures.* Why couldn't he be Brown or, even better, Dick. I smiled to myself, silently repeating, *Dickhead.* Then I looked up and returned his stare.

My head was really beginning to hurt. I started feeling queasy—the kind of queasy that ends up with you barfing on your shoes. But despite that awful feeling, I wasn't about to blow off this class. No matter how much of an a-hole this guy was, I'd totally lose it if I couldn't count on at least one music class each day.

"Actually, I've been playing the cello for almost my whole life," I said.

Mr. Whitehead sniffed. "I see. What's your name?" He looked down at his list. "Did you know that this class requires the approval of the instructor? If I don't agree to let you in, you can't be here. And you've already missed three weeks' work."

"I'm Jace Adams." I didn't feel like pointing out the obvious: that the reason this class was on my schedule was because it was already approved—by him.

When he found my name on the list, he looked up slowly and eyed me once again. "Oh, yes, now I remember. You're the *new* student."

"That's right," I said, feeling a sliver of hope.

"Someone—your mother, I presume—sent me a recording that's supposedly you playing."

"Yes," I said. "That's right."

"I must say," he declared slowly, turning to address the students seated in a half circle around him, "it was a most impressive performance. In fact, I've never heard a young cellist play better. How old are you?"

"Fourteen," I said.

"Really? Well, now that I'm looking at you, I'm sorry to say I have a hard time believing it was you playing. Did your mother inadvertently send me the wrong recording, *or*—?" He let the unfinished sentence hang in the air. By now, my head was throbbing and my eyes were watering, but I decided to take the bait, even though I knew it was a stupid thing to do.

"Or *what*?" I replied, my voice softly menacing. If he was going to accuse me of lying or, worse, accuse *my mom* of lying, I wanted him to say it out loud for everyone to hear. He got the point, because his face turned bright red. But before he had a chance to say anything else, the kid sitting in the first violin chair spoke up. I hadn't noticed, but it was Skinny Kid—I mean, Elvis.

"Why don't you just have him play for us, Mr. Whitehead?" he said pleasantly.

I was surprised; he didn't seem anything like the pathetic worm I'd defended that morning. Instead, he was sitting tall, with his back straight, as he spoke to the teacher in a direct, confident tone, his priceless violin ready. Mr. Whitehead pursed his lips for a moment, as if he was actually contemplating the suggestion. Then he gave me an evil smile.

"Indeed. Good suggestion, Mr. Goldberg." He motioned to a chair in front of the podium. I took a seat, and as I took my cello out of the case, I noticed a girl in the front row giving me a malicious smirk. She was holding a cello, too. She flipped her purple-streaked hair out of her eyes and leaned over to whisper something to the girl sitting next to her, and then they both laughed.

"Do you have some advice to share with the orchestra, Marcy?" Mr. Whitehead said.

"Oh, I was just telling Gretchen that I'd never seen such a cute little cello before. I was wondering if he got it at Toys'R'Us."

What? I was stunned by what she'd just said. I saw Elvis frown, but the rest of the kids in the orchestra laughed and so did that shit Whitehead. But what that girl'd just said was almost as bad as what almost happened that morning; she'd just dissed my cello! My mom may have found this cello in the back of a pawnshop, but Ruby was worth way more than any piece of crap musical instrument from some stupid toy store.

When the laughter faded, I knew there was only one thing left to do: I'd just play and show them exactly who Jace Adams was. First, I plucked the strings, adjusted a couple of pegs, and tried them again. I saw a faint smile cross Elvis's face. *Surprise, dude. I've done this a few thousand times before.*

"Anything in particular you'd like me to start with?" I asked, my voice shaking slightly in anger. "How about 'Big Pappa'? Or maybe 'Paid in Full'?" Mr. Whitehead started to sputter a reply, but Marcy beat him to it.

"How about Haydn? His *Cello Concerto No. 1*." I had to give her credit; she wasn't backing down.

"You mean the one in C major?"

Marcy's face darkened. "Is there another one?" she snipped.

"That's quite enough, Miss Gordon," Mr. Whitehead said, turning to me. "Why don't you just see what you can do with the C major scale?"

I settled myself and the cello, then drew the bow across the strings. Without really thinking, I let my fingers dance through the pattern of the C major scale. It'd been a few days since I'd played, but I could tell by the reaction of the kids in the orchestra that they were surprised by the rich cascade of notes that filled the room. I hit the last note, then jumped right into the Haydn concerto's finale, my bow and fingers beginning to move all on their own. That's how it'd always been: once I heard a melody or a song, it became a part of me, and the notes, well, they didn't really come from the musical instrument, but from somewhere deep inside me. I didn't even understand it, myself.

When I'd finished playing, the room was absolutely silent. And then I heard someone clapping. It was Elvis, his big red Afro bouncing as he applauded with enthusiasm. Then the rest of the orchestra joined in, raggedly at first, then getting louder. Meanwhile, Marcy just sat there, her face ashen. *Gotcha*. She couldn't look me in the eye, and I couldn't tell if she was ashamed of the way she'd treated me or pissed off because I could actually play. Before I could find out, I heard . . .

"Mr. A-dams!" The applause died out, and Mr. Whitehead was now standing with his arms crossed and his chin

up. Apparently, I'd done something unforgivable—I'd embarrassed him. It was a no-win situation.

"Please take a seat—at the back of the cello section,"
he said. "That was a surprising demonstration. But as you
know, anyone can solo; it takes a real musician to be part of
an ensemble."

"But, Mr. Whitehead," Marcy said, "he—he—"

"Yes?" Mr. Whitehead's voice snapped. "You have
something *more* you'd like to share with us?"

Marcy frowned. "No. I guess not."

I saw Elvis bite his lip and shake his head slightly. I
knew I wouldn't get more help from him today; he'd already done more than I could ever have expected. There
was nothing else to do, so I moved to the back row and
found a vacant chair next to a small kid who looked like he
still belonged in elementary school. He'd be my new music-
stand partner.

"Gosh, you were great," he squeaked as I sat down.
His voice hadn't changed yet, and he sounded like a talking
chipmunk.

"Uh-huh," I grunted.

"An orchestra is like a basketball team," Mr. Whitehead continued, glaring at me. "You people know something about basketball, don't you?"

You people? I'm sure to him I looked like just another
useless black teenager, end of story. But he didn't know
anything about me, and I'd never been like everyone else—
not even other black kids. Maybe that was the problem. He
didn't know that I was into surfing instead of basketball,
that I knew more about Laird Hamilton than LeBron James.

He just assumed he knew all about me, based just on how I looked. But I didn't say anything. I was just too tired and banged up to get pissed off. I closed my eyes and wondered if I was always going to feel this alone, if I'd ever actually belong anywhere.

It wasn't just freshman year that sucked; it was my whole life.

Did I mention that Mom and I were staying with my Aunt Bernice?

Ever since I could remember, I'd gotten to and from school on my own, no sweat. So walking the twelve blocks to Bernice's after school that day should have been a piece of cake—except for one thing: I was being followed. *Crap.* It had to be those morons from school. They were in what looked like an old classic Chevy Impala. I had to admit, they had good taste; it was sweet and in perfect shape, with chrome wheels, a purple paint job, and black-tinted windows. It'd been the car of choice for well-to-do gangbangers back in California.

After a few blocks, I wondered why they didn't try and get me. But they seemed content just to roll along, going no faster than I could walk, but staying close enough to keep me kind of freaked. Maybe they just wanted to check out where I lived so they could get me later?

I was in no mood to wait to find out what they were up to, so when I reached the next corner, I cut to the right and ran. I didn't stop at the end of the block, crossing the street without pausing or even looking, then was back on the sidewalk again. When I looked back over my shoulder, I saw that instead of following me, the purple car turned right quickly, exhaust spewing as it sped down the street. I self-consciously laughed in relief, then slowed to a normal walk. Maybe that whack on my head had done more damage than I thought. They probably weren't following me after all. More likely, it was just somebody delivering a pizza, wondering why that goofy kid was running off that way, like he was scared of something nobody else could see.

"What're you doin' home so soon?" Bernice growled as I walked up the front steps a few minutes later. She was sitting in a rocking chair on the porch, smoking a cigarette.

"Anyone ever mention those things'll kill you?" I asked.

She gave a rough laugh. "Yes, my first husband—or was it my second? Maybe both of those losers warned me about it. But since it pissed them off, I wasn't of any mind to stop. And now, I don't really care anymore."

"Oh" was all I could think to say. I pulled open the screen door, but she stopped me before I stepped inside.

"Drop your stuff and sit for a moment," she said. "We need to chat."

Chat? I barely knew her, but Bernice sure didn't seem to be the chatting type. She was at least six feet tall and probably tipped the scale easily at 250 pounds. She wasn't fat, either, just solid flesh and muscle. She wore her hair in dreadlocks that hung down below her shoulders, and Mom said she'd been a city bus driver for just about forever. Our first night in town, she'd told us a joke.

"You know the difference between a black female bus driver and a pit bull?"

My mom hadn't bothered to answer; she just sat back with half a smile and watched me. I thought about it, then guessed: "Lipstick?"

"Wrong," Aunt Bernice snarled. "A handgun." With that, they both screamed with laughter until tears streamed down their cheeks. And I'd wondered if this was Bernice's way of telling me she had a gun. If she did, I was sure it was no girl-gun, either. I'd expect at least a Glock or maybe a .357 Magnum revolver. That's the kind of piece my brother Derrick preferred.

I was still thinking about handguns when Bernice spoke to me again: "I don't want no funny stuff in my house."

"Funny stuff?" I repeated.

She took a drag of her cigarette and wrinkled her forehead. "You stupid or what? Do I need to spell it out?"

"Spell it out?" I repeated, sounding like a total ass.

She smacked me on the side of the head—and it was hard enough for me to see stars, given the abuse I'd already taken that day.

"Okay. Listen up, funny boy. First off, I don't want you bringing none of your skanky girlfriends around here, understand? I know what teenage boys are always thinking about; you just wanna get up their shirts or in their pants. I'll have none of your fornicating here in my house. Got it?"

I almost said, "Got it," but caught myself in time and just nodded. Bernice had that much right; I was no different from any other guy who liked girls. I'd even thought that Kari, the girl who now lived in Phoenix, might become my first *official* girlfriend. But we'd gone and moved before I even had a chance to, um, see where it might go. That's one of the problems with having a mom who's a serial mover.

"And no drugs," Bernice said, after pausing to take another drag on her cigarette. "I won't have none of that garbage in my house, and I won't have your momma go through what she went through with you know who."

I knew she meant Derrick. Mom had threatened me with a fate worse than death if I got messed up with drugs, alcohol, or gangs, and she reminded me about it at least once a week. I got the message.

I'd started wondering lately what Mom saw when she looked at me. I knew she didn't hate me or anything, but sometimes when I'd catch her staring at me, I'd wonder. Maybe she's not seeing me at all, but somebody else—like my old man or maybe my brother. They're both screw-ups, so maybe she's just waiting for me to prove that I'm no better, that I'm just another loser like them.

"And you'll have chores to do," Bernice continued. "As long as you're living here, you'll be pulling your own weight."

I nodded mechanically. But by then, I'd had just about enough of her crap. I didn't deserve this; what'd I ever done to her? I mean, she barely knew me. By now, my head was hurting again and I just wanted to go lie down somewhere. I thought about just telling her to bite me, but she might actually do it—or maybe just kick my ass. And since I tried to limit ass-kicking to just once a day, I kept my mouth shut.

"And I've been thinking about where you're gonna sleep. You can't stay on the couch in the living room."

"No, ma'am," I said, wondering what that meant even as I agreed with her.

"Your mom deserves a room of her own, and I'm not giving up my bedroom in my own house."

"Right. I wouldn't expect you to," I said sarcastically.

Then she sucked on her cigarette and narrowed her eyes. "So you'll be sleeping out back. You gotta problem with that?"

I closed my eyes and tried to imagine Bernice's backyard. There was a patch of grass and a garden against the back fence. On one side there was a garage, an alley, and a shed. I opened my eyes. "You mean that shed?"

"That's no shed," she said, blowing a jet of smoke over my head. "That's a guest house."

My day already sucked, and I didn't think it could get any worse, but I was wrong. And now my head hurt so much that my eyes were watering. I mean, that damn shed wasn't much bigger than a doghouse. The weather was decent right now, but how would it be in a few months—cold and raining or snowing?

"Yes, indeed," she purred, "I think that's the perfect place for you. Your mom agrees with me, too. A boy needs his space. You can make it cozy. I've got a space heater you can use for when it gets chilly. It'll be your own little Butch Cassidy hideout."

Emphasis on little, I thought. "What about going to the, um, you know, bathroom?" I said.

"You mean peeing? You aren't a dog. I expect you to

use the bathroom in the house like any housebroken child."
She closed her eyes and leaned back in her chair; I was dismissed.

My guest room was one of those pre-built sheds from Home Depot. It was supposed to look like a miniature barn from the outside, but I couldn't imagine any farmer painting his barn purple with bright yellow trim and topping it off with a green door. There was a narrow window near the eaves—just big enough to let in some light. I dropped my backpack and cello on the grass and stepped inside.

Bernice must have cleared it out while I was at school. I could tell she'd poured something strong on the floor, trying to cover up the smell. Whatever it was, it hadn't helped; I could still pick out the stench of rotting grass mixed with gasoline and oil, old weed killer, and fertilizer. It wasn't much better than a toxic waste site. *And I have to sleep here?*

But I guess it could've been worse. It wasn't as small as it looked from the outside; it was about ten feet long by eight feet wide. The walls and ceiling were covered with cheap fiberboard insulation, and about half the room was taken up by a cot that Bernice had topped with an ugly old mattress; I was probably better off not knowing where the stains on it came from. Some folded blankets had been stacked on the end of the bed, and next to it, she'd stuck a small white table with an old lamp and a small space heater, powered by an extension cord running from the house. I didn't see any place to put my clothes, but then I noticed some boxes under the cot and figured they were what Bernice must have planned for my storage—not that I had much, anyway.

I couldn't remember the last time I'd cried, but looking around at my new room, I admit I was close. Things had gone from bad to rotten. Here I was, living with my mom and her boy-hating aunt in yet another new city. I didn't have any friends, and I'd just had my ass kicked on the first day of school. My orchestra teacher was probably a card-carrying member of the Ku Klux Klan, and to top it off, I was going to be sleeping in a garden shed until Mom decided to take off again. I slumped onto the mattress, curled myself up, and closed my eyes.

Welcome home, sucker.

7

After I'd slept a while, I woke to the peaceful sound of rain on the roof. I rolled over and stared up at the shadows on the ceiling. Without looking at my watch, I could tell that at least a couple of hours had passed. My headache was gone, but my mouth tasted like crap. I needed to pee, and my stomach grumbled. I didn't bother to turn on the light next to my bed.

Before I moved another inch, I decided that I needed to figure out what to call this place. If it was going to be home for a while, there was no way I was going to call it a *shed*. *Guest house* didn't cut it, either. I thought about it for a while and then laughed. *Castle!* That'd be just perfect. A man's home—even if it's a shed—has gotta be his castle. And I knew Derrick would like that. I sat up slowly, remembering the beating I had taken. But except for some tenderness at the back of my neck, my head didn't seem like it was going to fall off or anything. I got up and stepped outside, turned my face up to the rain, and took a deep breath.

It is what it is. I repeated that phrase like a prayer, and for some reason, I felt better. At least we weren't living in my mom's car; we'd already done that a couple of times when she was between jobs. It wasn't fun, not even the first ten minutes. My stomach rumbled again, and I wondered what was for dinner. I crossed the wet lawn in my bare feet, went in through the back door, and called to my mom and then Bernice. When there was no response, I trudged into the kitchen and saw a note taped to the refrigerator.

Dear Lazy,

I'm at work. Your mom called to say she was working late, so you're on your own for dinner. Don't make a mess, and if you do, clean it up. Got it?

B

I crumpled the note and tossed it into the sink. *That Bernice is a gift that just keeps on giving.* I wondered where the nearest taco truck was parked. In L.A., taco trucks were always the best place to get a quick, cheap meal that was also good—three or four carne asada tacos—mmm. And that's when I got inspired. Yeah, I was hungry, but even more important, I was broke. I'd always managed to scare up a little dough by playing on the streets back in L.A., and it was easy and kind of fun. No reason I couldn't keep at it here in Seattle.

After the crappy day I'd just had, spending a few hours playing music without being bugged by anyone sounded just about perfect. And if I could make some money, too, even better. I knew there was a symphony in town, and maybe they were playing tonight. In that case, those symphony-goers were in for a real treat. Because in addition to hearing some internationally acclaimed superstar play with the orchestra, they'd also get to hear a street musician who happened to be one of the finest fourteen-year-old cellists anywhere—me.

I found some bread and peanut butter, and I quickly made two sandwiches. I uncrumpled Bernice's note and turned it over to write a note to my mom, telling her what I was doing; I didn't care if Bernice knew where I was. I ran out to my castle, grabbed my backpack, stuffed in a water bottle and the two sandwiches, then went back in the house and grabbed Ruby from the front closet. I made sure the front door was locked, then took off down the street to the nearest bus stop, the heavy cello case banging against me the entire way.

Since it was early evening, there weren't many people heading downtown; I got on a nearly empty bus and sat in the back, where I ate one of my sandwiches. After a couple of stops, I noticed one couple who seemed dressed up for a concert. They took one look at me and sat up front; I didn't think I was that scary-looking, but they were white and I was black, so it wasn't hard to figure out what that was about. Twenty minutes later, I hopped off the bus, guessing that the symphony was nearby.

The rain had stopped during the ride downtown, and the air smelled good. I stood on the sidewalk for a moment or two and looked around; nearby, a couple of college kids were sitting at a table under an awning outside a coffee shop. They glanced over at the cello case and then at me. *Now looks like a good time to ask for help.*

"Hey, can you tell me where the symphony plays?" I asked.

"Six blocks thataway," one of them said, pointing.

"Thanks. Do you know if they're playing tonight?"

One of the students replied. "Yeah, I think so," he said. "What've you got in there?"

"My cello."

"No shit?"

"No shit," I replied, more sharply than I intended.

"C'mon, man, chill. I was just wondering; with a case that size, I figured it might be a tenor sax or something. You know, like John Coltrane played."

"I thought about playing sax," I said, calmer. "Be easier than hauling this thing around. But you get more chicks playing the cello."

"For real?" he said.

"Yeah." I nodded, then headed towards the concert hall. Even though it'd rained earlier, it was warm now, with no wind. A steady stream of people passed me on the sidewalks—something you didn't see much in Southern California. I mean, why walk when you can drive? I checked my cheap Timex: 6:50. Call me stupid, but despite the day I'd had, I was excited to finally be doing something by myself. No rules or orders, no disappointments. And nobody in my face or on my case—just how I liked it. I jaywalked across the street and before long was standing across from Benaroya Hall, home of the Seattle Symphony.

I watched the street for a few minutes, trying to figure

out which direction people would be coming from on their way to the concert. But I was also scouting out any competition; street musicians have their own territory, and I knew it wasn't okay to play on someone else's turf. But I didn't see anyone else, and that surprised me. Back home, people were always playing music on the streets. Maybe that just meant we had more poor musicians back home. Or maybe it was the weather back there. Didn't matter to me. I was here, and I was going to take advantage of the situation.

I finally set up near the parking garage next to the hall. Since I'd left my portable stool at home, I'd sit on the steps to the garage. It didn't take long to get ready; I opened Ruby's case, took out the cello, and tossed in a few coins and the last dollar bill I had left; that's called priming the pump, and it prompts passersby to throw in some money, too.

Settled now on my step, I plucked the strings, checking to see if they were in tune, then made a few adjustments and started playing. It probably looked kinda strange. I mean, nothing weird about a young black guy dribbling a basketball, but a young black guy playing a cello? It wasn't exactly an everyday sight, especially in Seattle. But it wasn't weird to me. I thought the cello was the coolest-looking instrument around, and I loved the sound. The first time I pulled a bow across the strings, I was only six, but that amazing sound must have worked its way inside my soul from the first notes. Since that day, the cello's been the only thing that's never let me down.

I started off with a few warm-up exercises just to get

my fingers working, then moved on to some snippets from Bach's *Unaccompanied Cello Suites*. I was vaguely aware of people walking by; some even stopped to listen for a while. A few of them tossed money into my case, but I had no idea how much. That's the best thing about playing the cello—it takes me to some other place, and it gets to me like nothing else.

After I finished the Bach, I played a few popular songs. My old music teacher, Mr. Jensen, would have gone ballistic. "That's not fitting music for a cello," he'd scream whenever he caught me trying out something I'd heard on *American Idol* before my lesson. But he was back in L.A., so I did what I wanted. Since my mom was a big-time Beatles fan and played their CDs all the time, I'd picked up their songs from hearing them so much. I have a sticky brain when it comes to music; if I hear a tune once, I can usually play back the melody. So I also played some of the old jazz tunes I'd overheard coming from the apartment next door half a dozen moves ago. They were just as much a part of my DNA now as Bach and the Beatles. I mean, what the hell, why not?

So I played a little bit of everything, and I even sang along while I played. I have a decent voice, and I'd noticed that people gave me more cash when I sang, so it wasn't some kind of ego thing that got me doing it. Nah—it was all about the money.

As the last notes of "Lullaby of Birdland" echoed up and down the dark streets, I finally looked up and blinked; it always feels like I'm coming out of a trance when I stop playing. The sidewalk was deserted, except for this guy in rags who was leaning against a battered grocery cart piled high with all of his worldly possessions.

"You're in my spot," he said, his voice a deep growl.

Man, oh man. Now the proverbial crap was about to hit the fan. I glanced at my cello case on the ground, figuring that if worse came to worse, I'd grab Ruby and whatever money I could scoop up, then take off running. It wouldn't be the first time I'd lost a case that way.

"Sorry," I said. "I'm new here. . . . I didn't know this was your place."

His attitude changed so suddenly, it took me by surprise. "No sweat, no sweat, my man," he said. "I have a special permit to play here from the Seattle Police Department, honorable Mayor Joseph PDQ Bach Smith, and Mr. Vladimir Putin of the ex-Soviet Union, USSR. But you are such an awesome player, of the quality and caliber I have never heard before, that I am honored that the voice of God brought you to this place of shelter and sacrifice."

The words tumbled out with a rhythm that was almost musical. I had no idea what he was talking about, so I said the first thing that came to my mind: "Thanks, man. I'm honored to be playing in your place."

He gave me a hard stare, wondering if I was making fun of him. When he realized I wasn't, a big, beautiful grin burst across his face. "Thank *you*, young sir!" he said. "You're an awesome and respectful son of God, Jehovah, and Buddha. So what the hell is your name?"

"Jace."

I watched him squat down, pull a piece of chalk from his pocket, and write a few words on the street. I saw him add my name in letters large enough for me to see, and then, with an orange piece of chalk, he circled my name with the jagged flames of a sun. Then he spoke again:

"Well, Mr. Jace. Someday I expect to be reading about you playing with the Supernatural National Symphony Orchestra of Washington State and Seattle."

"Yeah, right," I said quietly.

He heard me. "Don't go disbelieving me," he replied sharply. "I got the gift."

"What gift is that?" When he smiled, I realized he'd been waiting for me to ask.

"I know players. And you, my man, are a player. I can spot them. Mr. Jimi Hendrix—I spied him out first. The Wilson girls—I spied them out first. Mr. Kurt Cobain—I spied him out first. Uh-huh. It's true."

I didn't know what to say. "Thanks," I mumbled.

"Sorry I don't have any money for you," he said.

"That's all right," I replied. And I meant it. One look at the collection of rags and old blankets he was wearing, and his face—which looked like an old catcher's mitt in need of a shave—and I knew my life wasn't all that bad compared to his. Then I saw his eyes slip out of focus and he started pawing at a pocket.

"Hey, I do got a coupla these," he said. He came close enough for me to smell him, so I held my breath. Then he handed me a slip of paper. As I reached out, he grabbed my hand, shaking it like he was trying to jack up a car. "Pleased to make your acquaintance, Jace. Maybe I'll see you around sometime. You can call me Sir Lionel."

"All right, um, Sir Lionel," I said, looking closely at

the paper. It was a coupon for a free cheeseburger at McDonald's. I looked at the expiration date, which had passed a year ago, but I didn't have the heart to tell him. "Thanks, Lionel—"

"That's *Sir* Lionel," he interrupted with a guttural yell. He said it with such passion, I wouldn't have been surprised to see him pull a knife out of his pocket and come at me. What a complete freak this guy was.

"Uh, sorry, Sir Lionel," I said, backing up and trying to keep my voice from shaking. "But you know, I don't feel right about taking it. So why don't we trade? I'll take the coupon, and why don't you take this?" I pulled a five-dollar bill out of the wad in my left hand and pressed it into his hand.

"Why, I couldn't do that," he said, looking closely at the bill.

"Okay then," I said, thinking quickly, "how about not just a trade but a down payment on advertising. I'll be playing down here again sometime—if that's okay with you, it being your spot and all. And when I do, you can handle my advertising—like what you wrote just now."

He chuckled, suddenly looking and sounding as sane as anyone, which made me wonder if it was all just an act. "Nice try, kid, but I won't argue with U.S. Grant," he said, snatching the bill from my hand. "Next time, I'll give you one of my special blessings. You look like you could use my help." With that, he pushed off down the street, talking quietly to himself.

I need help? Taken a look at yourself lately, man? But there was no point in arguing with a nutcase. I put Ruby and my bow away, pulled on my backpack, and grabbed my cello case. I could see a Mickey D's sign glowing a couple of blocks away and headed towards it. After I got my food, I sat by myself at the back, where I ate two cheeseburgers, a super-size fries, and topped it off with hot coffee and plenty of cream and sugar.

As I sipped my coffee, it occurred to me that in some ways, maybe my life wasn't any better than Sir Lionel's. Sure, I wore nicer, cleaner clothes and I wasn't a nut, but my life was far from normal. I mean, I should have been at home tonight—in a real home—and with my dad. You know, maybe out in his shop, working on his car or something like that, and my mom'd be talking on the phone with her friends. And instead of sitting by myself in a McDonald's, I'd be watching TV or maybe being a couch potato and playing video games with my brother; everything would be so fine. I'd be part of a normal family.

But instead, here I was, just another loser: I had an aunt who hated me, a mom who could barely run her own life, let alone do much for me. I'd just wrecked my first day at a new school, and now I was downtown, trying to scare up some pocket money by playing like a beggar on the streets in another new city. I shook my head and smiled with regret. And you know what? The more I thought about it, the more I thought it was actually kind of funny. It had to be, since I wasn't about to cry in public.

I was tempted to head home, but by the time I finished my coffee, the thought of the extra twenty or thirty bucks I could make playing after the concert won out. I headed back, and as I set up, I watched for Sir Lionel, but he was nowhere in sight. This time, I picked the entryway of an office building across from where I'd been earlier. I figured this spot would give me a chance to play for a different crowd going in the opposite direction when the concert ended.

When the first few people began to leave, I started playing. I could vaguely sense people passing by, some stopping to listen but most just continuing on their way. As I played one song after another, barely stopping between pieces, I tuned out everything around me. I felt like the only thing not moving in the entire universe, with everything else swirling around me like stars in the sky.

At one point, I surfaced from my musical trance long enough to focus on the faces before me, and that's when I saw Marcy standing there, her eyes widening in surprise as she recognized me. She was all wrapped up in a big coat and sandwiched between her mom and dad. They all watched me, and it made me feel like an animal on display at the zoo. I felt my cheeks getting hot as I imagined what she'd be blabbing tomorrow at school: "The new kid, Jace Adams, is so poor; I saw him playing for money on the street." That was all I'd need, on top of everything else. It's not like I'd gotten such a great start at school so far.

Screw you, I thought, then switched mid-measure from Bach to a popular hip-hop song, saying the words to myself under my breath. Halfway through it, I glanced up, ready to challenge Marcy with a stare, but she was already gone. The song was driving the rest of the crowd away, too, with their thoughts easy enough to read on their faces: *black ghetto punk.*

I played for another fifteen minutes, long enough for Marcy and her parents to be long gone. And I'd made a decent pile of bills for myself—before I'd switched to hip hop, at least. Combined with what I'd made earlier, I'd probably taken in forty or fifty bucks—not bad. I gathered it up, stuffed it back into my cello case with Ruby, and then headed for the bus stop.

I saw my bus pull up to the curb when I was still about two blocks away. I broke into a run, wrestling with my cello case as best as I could, and I'm sure it didn't look pretty. *Whatever.* I got close enough to see the bus driver watching me in the mirror. He waited until I was half a block away, then closed the door and took off. *Damn!* Being new to the area, I had no idea when the next bus would come, but at this time of night, after 10 p.m., it'd be a long wait.

And that's where my mom found me—sitting there on the bench, chin on my chest, staring blankly at my feet. I glanced up at the sound of her voice. She'd pulled her car up in front of the bus stop and was leaning across the seat, talking to me through the open window.

"So you want a ride," she said, "or are you set on riding the bus back to Bernice's?"

"I've always liked buses," I said without thinking; that made her eyebrows go up, which jolted my brain to start working. "But a ride would be fine," I said. She pushed open the door, then sat back behind the wheel and watched me lay the cello case on the backseat and then get in beside her.

As I shut the door, I noticed a purple low rider idling a block away and felt a sudden flush of panic. How long had it been there? It looked just like the car I thought was following me home from school earlier. Was it a coincidence? I didn't believe in them, so I locked the door. As Mom pulled out into traffic, I kept my eye on the purple car. When it stayed put, I slumped down in the seat and let out an audible sigh.

"You okay?" she asked.

"No worries," I said.

"How'd you do tonight?"

"Don't know. I haven't counted it up yet."

"Dinner?"

"I ate at Mickey D's," I said.

"Me, too," she said. "You know, you could call me for a ride."

She was right. I could've called her. And maybe she'd have come to pick me up. Or maybe she'd have been mad that I called her. That was the thing with my mom—I never knew which one I'd get: the once-in-a-while, randomly nice mom or the grouchy, angry one who'd jump down my throat and not want to be bothered. It could go either way.

I shrugged. "I didn't want to bug you on your first day at work."

"I had a message from school, but I didn't get a chance to call back. Anything I should be worrying about?" I could feel her eyes on me.

"Nah," I said, relaxing against the back of the seat.

She'd used the word *worry*, but I'm not sure she had any idea what that actually meant. She didn't seem to worry when we lived in Dallas, where Derrick and I made pocket change by hustling drunks for aluminum cans. She didn't seem to worry later on, when we switched from recycling to playing music. Derrick joined me on a cheap Casio keyboard; we weren't very good, but we were cute—and people were willing to pay for cute.

"You make me feel like I'm a bad mother or something," she snapped.

"That's not what I meant," I said.

"You back-talking me, young man?"

"No, ma'am." I crossed my arms and stared out the window.

"This isn't like where we came from. I knew there were people watching out for you there."

I didn't bother to say anything; it'd just be a waste to argue with her. Instead, I squinted and began to play Ruby in my mind, the passing trees adding rhythm to the accompaniment as we blew past.

"You hear me, young man?"

I grunted in agreement as I imagined my fingers moving to play different notes. I'd been forced to grow up fast, though I doubt Mom saw it that way. It was all I knew, so for me, it was normal. And it meant I was probably more independent than most fourteen-year-olds. I didn't ask her for anything, and she only asked me to keep out of trouble—not because of anything bad that might happen to me but because of the hassle it would cause her. Somehow, everything always ended up being about her. And I could tell that this was about to become one of those times.

"I'll be working a lot of hours at this new job," she went on. "I need to make a good impression, you know. But next time you take off in the evening and I'm not around, you call me and tell me where you're going to be."

"All right."

"So how'd your first day go?" Okay, now she was going to try and be the good mom. I thought back to the fight, then sleepwalking through my first classes, and then getting called out by Mr. Whitehead in orchestra class. I thought about Bernice's lecture and then finding out about sleeping in a garden shed. I glanced over at my mom. It must have been the darkness, but for the first time, I realized she wasn't so young anymore. The shadows and lines that flickered across her face as we passed under the streetlights made her almost look like a stranger.

"No worries, Mom," I said softly. "I got this starting a new school thing down cold."

"Good." She exhaled with obvious relief. "So there's nothing to that message from your school?"

"Nah. I think they do that for all the new students."

She settled lower into her seat. "That's what I figured. You ready to start cello lessons again? I can ask around, make some calls. . . . "

"I don't know. . . . " I let my voice trail off.

"What do you mean?"

"I think I need a little break from lessons right now." I half expected Mom to jump down my throat about the lessons, but instead she just nodded. And that was that.

Bernice was still out when we got to her house. Mom disappeared down the hall, and I heard her close her bedroom door; if she'd said good night, I missed it. As I stood there in the dark house, I realized that something had changed between us. Somewhere on the ride back from downtown, whatever had still connected me and my mom was lost. Maybe it was when she didn't yell at me for not wanting to take lessons—like she didn't care what I did anymore. Or maybe it was what she said about putting in a lot of hours at her new job, like it was her way of saying I'd be on my own from now on. I wondered if she'd noticed what had happened—or even cared.

I heard her turn on some music—that was something that'd never change. Music and my mom always went hand in hand. Her cell phone rang, and I heard her laugh. I could tell by the sound of her voice that she was talking to a man. We'd been in town just two or three days, and she was already working it with some guy—that had to be a new record. I gave it two months max, and then we'd be hitting the road again. I shook my head.

My eyes burned as I walked down the hallway without seeing, then turned into the kitchen and kept going. I pushed open the back door and stepped outside.

"It is what it is," I whispered to the night.

8

I had to take a pee—that's what woke me up. I tried to ignore the increasing pressure, but finally I gave up and stuck my head outside. The sky was bright with stars, despite competition from the city lights. To the east was a faint, pink glow—dawn already on its way.

I looked across the lawn to the back of the house. All the lights were off, and it was probably locked up, too. No way was I going to go bang on the back door and beg to be let in, so I slipped into my flip-flops and shuffled over to the fence. I'd noticed a row of carefully tended plants—roses, I think, but it didn't really matter—not for what I had in mind. *Ahhhh, take that, Auntie dear*, I thought as I pissed on the nearest plant. Though with my luck lately, watering them this way would probably make them grow into award-winning specimens with pancake-sized flowers rather than shrivel up and die.

It was too cold to be outside, so when I was done, I took one more look at the sky and went back into my shed. But now, I couldn't sleep; my brain had clicked into gear, spinning from one weird thing to the next, finally landing

on the loose cash I'd left lying around. That was stupid—
really stupid; if some punk all high on crank decided to kick
in the door to my shack—I mean, castle—and steal all the
money, it'd be my own fault for not hiding it.

I flicked on a light, rolled out of bed, and searched for
a place to hide my stash. There wasn't much to work with:
the floor was a solid sheet of plywood, and the roof and
walls were covered with sheets of insulation. Any hole I
made would stand out like a neon sign. I could hollow out
a book, but that'd only work if nobody started tossing things
around. What about the mattress? Nah, that'd be the first
place thieves would look. The bed frame? It was made out
of metal tubing and covered with flaking black paint, and
the ends of the legs had plastic caps on the feet. I lifted up
one end of the cot and pried the cap off—perfect. The leg
was hollow and about the diameter of an empty toilet paper
tube. Nobody'd ever think to look there; at least I didn't
think so.

I'd picked up a decent wad of bills from playing the
night before, but I hadn't bothered to count it. And I hadn't
told my mom. No sense giving her any idea about how
much I'd made; when I'd saved a little money in the past,
she'd find out and then "borrow" it with a promise to pay
me back. But my mom makes lots of promises, and these
were like most of the others she made. I was still waiting for
her to repay me for all those loans.

I opened up Ruby's case and dumped the bills and
coins onto my bed. When I'd played by myself on the
streets in California, I'd always gotten a nice mix of dollar
bills along with a few fives and tens. For a while, I thought

people chipped in because they liked my playing. I even said as much one night while my brother and I were sharing a can of Spaghetti O's.

"You're kidding me, right?" Derrick said.

I swallowed a spoonful and frowned.

"I mean," he said, "you actually think people give you money because you're good or you're cute or whatever?"

I didn't like the direction this conversation was going, but I looked up to Derrick, so instead of hitting him with my spoon, I scowled and said, "I dunno."

"Look, dummy, you're playing better and all, but the reason all these people give you money is because you are a cute little black kid playing a cello and they feel sorry for you. And whether you like it or not, they give you a few dollars to keep from worrying that you'll follow them to their car and pull a knife on them or something."

"I'd never do anything like that," I retorted.

I noticed a gleam in his eyes. "I know that and you know that, but they don't."

I had to think about that for a moment. "So either they're scared, or they feel sorry for me?"

Derrick nodded.

"All of them?"

Derrick shrugged. "Does it matter?"

I took another spoonful of Spaghetti O's. "No. Guess not," I said. "Money is money."

"You got that right." There was an edge to his words that only later, when he was in prison, did I come to understand.

Money is money, I thought as I stared at the crumpled pile of bills and change. Then I began to count, starting with the coins. I got $4.20—not bad. Next, I unfolded the bills, spreading them out on the floor and rearranging them like a bank cashier, making sure they were same side up and pointed in the same direction. Usually, I sorted the different denominations into separate piles, but there were only ones in this batch—until I came to the last bill, which had a paper clip attached to it.

I picked it up to take a closer look. I blinked and then rubbed my eyes: there had to be a mistake. When I looked again, I let out a whoop and jumped to my feet, scattering everything across the floor. Ben Franklin was staring back at me from a hundred-dollar bill. "Nice to meet you, Mr. Franklin," I said. Shaking my head, I held the bill up to the light, just to make sure.

And that's when I noticed that the paper clip attached a business card to the bill. I slipped off the clip and was tempted to toss the card aside; it wouldn't be the first time somebody had used money to try and sell me on religion. But instead of that, there was a name and phone number printed on the card:

Dr. Aldo Majykowski
Bainbridge Island, Washington
(206) 555-4671
Majykowskiman@uofw.edu

And on the other side was a neatly printed message in blue ink:

Want to make a difference? Call me.
Dr. Majykowski

If I hadn't been so tired, I'd have laughed. *Me, make a difference? What a joke.* My life was a mess, and if this guy knew how much of one, he'd want his $100 back. I tossed the card on the table next to my bed and yawned. Now I was ready for some sleep. But first, I stacked the bills together, rolled them into a tight bundle, and slipped it into the bed frame's leg. Then I snapped the plastic cap back in place and climbed onto the mattress, flicking off the light. That was all I remembered; I was asleep that fast.

I guess there were some benefits to sleeping above a fat wad of bills, because I woke to the sound of birds and light streaming through my dust-streaked window. I huddled under my blanket for a few minutes, then finally got up, pulled on sweats and flip-flops, and staggered across the wet lawn to the back steps. I found the back door open, and as I stepped inside, Bernice looked up. She was sipping coffee and reading the newspaper.

"Better get your ass in gear, or you're going to be late for school," she snipped.

"Good morning to you, too, Aunt Bernice," I snapped, before I had a chance to stop myself. *Crap, now she's going to kick my ass.*

She took a sip of coffee, her dark eyes watching me over the edge of the cup. "Good morning, sunshine," she said in a singsong voice, with just the hint of a smile. Then she scowled again. "That better?"

I shrugged. "Where's Mom?" I asked.

"She was up and out early."

"Trying to make a good impression," I muttered to myself.

"Nothing wrong with that," Bernice snapped. "Fresh towels in the closet next to the door as you go in the bathroom. Use one for a week before you toss it in the laundry basket. I'll show you later how to use the washer and dryer in the basement. I have no intention of being your maid, and I 'spect your momma won't want to, either."

I nodded back at her.

"Just a few kitchen rules we should go over. Help yourself to anything you want for breakfast, and clean up after you're done. Stay away from my booze and my cigarettes, and we'll get along just peachy."

"That all?"

Bernice lit a cigarette, waved the match in the air to put it out, then placed the smoking matchstick in the ashtray. "I heard you're a good musician," she said.

I shrugged.

"What do you play?"

"Cello."

"Jello?"

"No, CHELL-O," I said.

Bernice squinted as smoke pecked at her eyeballs. "You trying to be a smart ass?"

"No, ma'am."

"That's good. 'Cause I hate smart asses. My first husband turned out to be a smart ass."

"Yeah?"

"Yeah. And he's dead now." She thought that was

funny. I hadn't considered psycho as an attribute of my Aunt Bernice, but now I reconsidered.

"And one other thing," she growled.

"What's that?"

"Your Mom and I talked this morning before she left the house, and she agreed with me. You need to try out for a sport."

"I'm a surfer," I said.

Bernice snorted. "Everybody knows black men don't surf. Just like everybody knows that black men don't swim—at least, not very well."

"That's just a load of racist bull—"

"Watch your tongue," Bernice interrupted, "or you'll find me slapping you with it.

"The waves don't care what color you are," I said.

"What was that?"

"Nothing."

"That's right, nothing. Like I was saying, you gotta go out for a sport—a real one. Not surfing or skateboarding or playing video games. You know anything about football?"

I shook my head. "I don't play football," I said. "Besides, practices started a few weeks ago. I'd be way behind. And I can't take a chance on hurting my hands."

Bernice glanced at me over the newspaper and then shook her head in disgust. "Then I guess that means you're gonna have to go out for cross-country."

"Why?"

"Because you're going to run. African runners are the best in the world for long distances. Bet you didn't know that, did you?"

I shrugged.

"Well, in addition to your Swedish blood . . . "

"Irish."

"Whatever. In addition to that, you got the DNA of some tough-as-nails Africans in you." She put the paper down and looked at me. "They're tall and wiry, like you. I bet you can run for miles and hardly get winded."

I shrugged again.

"Thought so. Well, then, it's settled: you'll go out for cross-country. And I don't want to see you around here before five in the evening. Got it? And remember, no drugs or fornicating. I sniff some strange girl in this house, they're going to be calling you an *it* instead of a *him*. You understand what I'm saying?"

That's when I noticed that my hands were clenched, like I really wanted to let Aunt Bernice have it. I was already sick of her hating me. And then it dawned on me: *She wants you gone, man.* I didn't know where that thought came from, but I felt my face flush. Sure, that was it, and it made sense. That's why she'd been riding my ass—she wanted me outta here. Mom was her niece, but me? I was just the kid who was wrecking my mom's life; like father, like son.

"Hey, dummy? What's wrong with you?" She was staring at me.

I didn't bother to answer. I turned and headed for the bathroom, careful to lock the door. Then I stood under the shower until the water was cold. When I was done, Bernice was gone.

9

Eventually, my life settled into a routine. I hardly ever saw my mom; she was usually gone by the time I got up and didn't get back until long after I'd turned in. When I was younger and she had to leave early, she'd always leave a note for me on the kitchen counter, usually with a smiley face and a word or two about having a great day. Or sometimes it was just the letters "L" and "U," for *love you*.

When she didn't have a boyfriend, Friday night was our date night—just me and her and Derrick. We'd go to Chuck E. Cheese or maybe McDonald's, and then we'd find a movie. And for a few hours, I could imagine life as something better than it actually was. Maybe she could, too. But now that I was fourteen, I guess she figured she'd done what she could and I didn't need any of that kind of mush. *Whatever.*

Meanwhile, every day or two, I'd run into Bernice at breakfast. She'd be sitting in the chair by the window, smoking a cigarette, drinking a huge cup of coffee, and reading the *Seattle Times*. She'd usually grunt something in greeting, and I'd respond with a word or two, then make some toast, grab a banana, and duck back outside.

Soon September turned into October. In Southern California, it wouldn't have made any difference. But here in Seattle, the trees were blazing with orange, yellow, and red. Everything was so bright and colorful, it reminded me of a Pixar cartoon. This was my first experience with fall; I'd never experienced four seasons before. In Southern California, people joked that there were only two: summer and not quite summer. I didn't think it was that funny, but there you go.

Most mornings, I'd scrounge up some breakfast and eat outside, sitting in my doorway on an old lawn chair I'd found behind Bernice's house. There, I could listen to the birds and the distant traffic rushing into town. Bernice was my time clock. Every morning at 7:43, I'd hear her running the water in her kitchen; that was my signal to finish eating, pull on some clothes, grab my backpack and cello, and head off for school, which started at a quarter after eight.

Elvis, still grateful to me for saving his violin, I guess, had tried a few times to be friends. He invited me to eat lunch with him and that girl, Marcy, and some other kids from the orchestra, but he finally got tired of me saying no and gave up; he hadn't asked me in over a week, and it was just as well. Mom and I'd be moving again soon anyway, so what was the point of making friends?

About once a week, when I got tired of being by myself during lunch, I'd stop in to say hello to Mrs. Allen, the school nurse. We didn't talk about anything important, but once she told me that she and her husband took their two kids up to the San Juan Islands on their sailboat, where they'd sleep on the boat or head for a deserted beach, pitch a tent, and sleep on the sand. It sounded nice. She asked me about living in California, and then, almost before I realized it, I was telling her about all the moving around we did and that I played music on the streets to make money.

"When did you start doing that?" she asked.

"I was six, and my older brother and I played music together. I was pretty good, even back then."

"I'm sure you were," she said, thoughtfully. "I'm sure you were."

Despite the mess of my first day, I was doing a good job of becoming invisible—better than I had at most of my other schools. Even Mr. Whitehead, the evil orchestra teacher, seemed to have forgotten about me; so I kept my head down, my mouth shut, and played the music, careful to follow Marcy's and the second cello's lead.

Turns out, the school orchestra was decent. In fact, it was a lot better than decent; it was probably the best school orchestra I'd ever played in. And Marcy was a fine player—not as good as me, for sure—but good. I'd also noticed she wasn't bad-looking; I liked the purple streaks in her hair, which she changed to red a few weeks later. I even thought about telling her—about being a pretty good player, I mean—but I could never think of a good way to say it without sounding like a moron. Yeah, I'm a wimp sometimes.

I'd followed Bernice's orders and gone out for cross-country, too. Mr. Ford was the coach, and he gave me a big grin when I showed up. It reminded me of the kind of greeting a lion might give a gazelle just before he takes his first bite. I kept hoping he'd say I was too late to go out for it, but it turned out he was hard up for runners. He even waived the fifty-dollar sports fee when I said I couldn't pay it and ignored my forgery of Mom's signature on the bottom of the permission form.

I shook my head no when he asked me if I had any running shoes, and even that didn't stop him. He reached into a battered cardboard box and handed me a pair of used Nike running shoes that smelled like they had been taken from a dead man. But they fit; at least that dead guy's feet were the right size.

No one was ever home when I walked through the front door each day after school, which was never before five. Bernice was already on her shift, and Mom always worked late, so I'd eat dinner by myself, take care of any homework, and practice the cello. I know it sounds weird, but playing Ruby was about the only time I ever felt normal. I always played in my room, so I'd open up the castle door for fresh air and work through the old music I remembered, practicing the fingering and bowing until it was as perfect as I could make it without a teacher.

Most of the kids I had known were into hip hop and rap, but even that depended on who you hung with; not everybody listened to everything. Like, it was okay for someone like me to listen to Jay-Z or even Michael Jackson, but R.E.M. and Coldplay weren't supposed to be the kind of music a black guy listens to. Likewise, most of the stoners were into metal, the Goths had their own music, and so did the Latinos and Asians, the cheerleaders, and so on. But me, I couldn't care less what people thought I was supposed to like—I was into all kinds of music, and I guess that made me even more of a freak.

Meanwhile, every three or four days, I hopped the bus downtown, timing my trips to coincide with evening events at the concert hall; Mom and Bernice didn't seem to care where I was going, as long as I left a note. I can't say I loved these sidewalk gigs, either; even though I had absolutely zero friends, there were plenty of other things I'd rather be doing. I kept it up because I needed the money. I'd learned long ago that you could never have too much of the stuff. I couldn't really put my finger on why I felt like I needed to stash away a lot of cash, but my radar kept going off. Everything seemed just fine on the surface, but somewhere out there, something wasn't quite right. I don't know if it had something to do with Bernice or Mom or if it was just me, but my gut was telling me to watch out. And so I did the best thing I could to get ready for whatever was coming at me—I squirreled away cash.

When I played downtown, I always set up in the same place as the first time. It was the perfect spot for the early concertgoers to hear me. After they were all inside, I'd grab something to eat at Mickey D's, then hop the bus back to Bernice's. I found out it didn't pay to hang around and play afterwards; people just wanted to get home.

Sir Lionel always showed up just as I was packing up to leave. I'm not sure where he was while he listened—maybe just someplace off in the shadows. But he always had something to say about how I played or the music I'd selected. The guy may have been homeless, but he sure knew his music. So I paid attention to what he said about my work—and I made sure to always call him Sir Lionel so he wouldn't go off on me again. He said that the last time I'd played, he'd heard people talking about me, wondering who I was and what my story was.

"What people?" I asked, thinking record producer or maybe those three bullies from school.

"You know," Sir Lionel said, twitching his shoulders as if bugs were biting him.

"No, I don't know. What people are asking about me? Was my mom down here looking for me or something?"

"No, indeed. It was a messenger from the king, and he said he'd heard about you and wanted to know how you were doing."

"What did you tell this, um, messenger?" I asked. I usually played along with him, but half the time I couldn't tell if Sir Lionel was actually in the present or not. I mean, he'd be standing there in front of me sometimes, but I could tell by what he was saying or from the look on his face that he was off somewhere, like Mars—or someplace even scarier.

"I told the messenger to tell the king that you are the gifted child, and much greatness will come to the king and to this city, Seattle, Washington State, United States of America, and Earth, Solar System, Milky Way Galaxy, when you truly embrace your gift."

The words rushed out, and I was momentarily stunned into silence. I wished I'd been able to record it; the way he'd said it sounded like the lyrics of a song.

"Well," I said, finally, "thank you very much for watching out for me, Sir Lionel. I am in your—" I tried to think of a word that a knight might appreciate. "Yes, I am in your debt."

"A debt of honor is the best kind," Sir Lionel said, with a twinkle in his eyes. And then he was off, pushing his cart down the street, an old coffee bag wrapped around his head like a turban.

"Good night to you, too," I said quietly. So far, nobody'd tossed another hundred-dollar bill into the Jace Adams Relief Fund, but when I played, I'd usually get home with at least thirty or forty dollars, and that was enough to get me through the week. I mean, it's not like I had any serious habits or anything. Just coffee and playing the cello—and maybe sometimes thinking about Marcy.

10

It was a Saturday night, the last weekend of October. Mom called to say she was eating at the office, so I was on my own, as usual. I heated up some noodles, added some peanuts and a little Tabasco sauce, and ate that for dinner, using plastic chopsticks from the cupboard. Then I cleaned up and went out to my castle, where I flopped down on my bed in the dark. For a minute, I thought about playing my cello; since I had absolutely no life in Seattle, I'd been playing several hours a day. And just to be clear, I don't practice, I play. I mean, you don't practice breathing, do you? Playing's the same thing for me.

I yawned in the darkness and realized I didn't feel like being alone—not tonight. Even if it only meant being around strangers, I wanted human company. I flicked on the light, threw on a sweatshirt, and pulled on my running shoes. With apologies to Ruby, I headed out and started walking, without any specific direction in mind. Bernice's house was in a nice neighborhood about three blocks from Green Lake; it was an area of older homes fifteen minutes from downtown, all fixed up, with green lawns and big

leafy trees. Nearly everyone I'd seen around the neighborhood looked white, drove fancy Japanese or European cars,
and seemed to have big dogs that they were forever walking, one hand trying to hang onto the leash and the other
holding a bag filled with dog poop—not exactly my defi-
nition of fun.

I wondered how Bernice managed to live in such an
upscale neighborhood; I was pretty sure bus drivers didn't
make all that much money. But what did I know? Everyone has secrets, and I'm sure Bernice had a few. I wouldn't
have been surprised to find out she had a couple of ex-husbands buried in her backyard. Now, the thought of sleeping
a few feet away from human worm food should have
freaked me out, but I laughed out loud instead. That made
a spiky-haired man across the street look up at me and
scowl behind his designer glasses. He looked like some
wannabe actor, standing there under the streetlight, trying
to look dignified while his huge dog took a dump on somebody's lawn.

"Make sure you pick that shit up," I said, feeling reck-
less. "I'm checking when I come back. And if you don't, I
know where you live, so you don't want to mess with me."
I was lying, but he didn't know that; I broke into a trot before he had a chance to respond.

Soon I was on the path that circled Green Lake; it was
really more of a pond than a lake, though. Maybe a long
time ago, this lake was surrounded by forests and was home
to all sorts of beavers and otters. But now, it looked like
something you'd see at Disneyland, with too many bright
lights glittering along the shoreline. All it needed was a fake

waterfall at one end, some plastic flamingos, and a few mechanical hippos at the other, and I'd feel like I was right back in Southern California. I guess tacky things turn up no matter where you go.

But despite all that, at least I wasn't alone. There were plenty of strangers all around me, and I slipped into the steady flow of joggers, walkers, and the occasional rollerblader. I pulled up the hood of my sweatshirt and tried not to think about anything aside from putting one foot in front of the other, my stride keeping pace with the rest of the pack.

At first, I figured the music I was hearing came from somebody's car. But this wasn't the kind of music you usually hear blasting from a car; I mean, it wasn't exactly some guy rapping out words with a lot of boom. Nope, this was music that was close to perfect, and I also knew it was composed by somebody who I'd have liked to meet—Bach. Too bad he'd been dead about 200 years.

I looked around, trying to find the source of the music, and that's when I realized that while my brain had been shut off, I'd nearly circled the lake. And before me, in the middle of a huge lawn, was a round glass building, all lit up, with people inside, eating and dancing. Wanting to get a better look, I walked across the dark lawn, up to the edge of the building, and stopped just outside the splash of light. Then I stood there, closed my eyes, and listened to the awesome sounds of violin and cello. This kind of music was my world, and it was very easy to get lost in it. And for a while, I guess I did.

When the music finally stopped, the sound drifted

away to polite applause. Then I opened my eyes and noticed the musicians for the first time: Marcy and Elvis. I guess I wasn't surprised. I knew they were good; I just hadn't realized how good. They turned in my direction, holding hands and bowing. I felt a stab of jealousy. Yeah, it was partly because they were holding hands. But the real reason was that I had to play on the street, while they got to perform in this cool glass hall. And there it was—the real difference between us.

It is what it is.

I'm not sure what made Marcy look outside when she reached down to get her cello case, but that's when she saw me. It was my fault, too. As I'd been pulled closer by their music, I'd drifted out of the shadows and into the patch of light just outside the windows. And before I had a chance to react, I saw her eyes widen as she turned and said something to Elvis. I thought he'd ignore me; after all, I hadn't been very friendly. Actually, I'd been a real jerk. But instead, he looked up and smiled at me. And then he did something that totally shocked me: he motioned for me to come inside.

I pointed at my chest, asking if he meant me and not someone behind me. Elvis nodded and motioned again, and Marcy nodded, too. Before I had a chance to take off, Elvis quickly opened a door, leaned out, and said, "Hey, Jace. So what did you think?" All those times I'd ignored him and refused to eat lunch together didn't seem to matter one bit.

"You were good," I said. "Very good."

"For real?"

"Yeah. It sounded great—even from out here."

"Thanks. We do it for fun—and get a little money, too."
He winked.

I nodded and pulled up the hood of my sweatshirt.
"Well, I gotta go."

"We're done, and now we get to eat. Why don't you
come and have something with us? There's tons of food." I
glanced over and noticed that Marcy was fumbling with her
cello.

"Naw, I really should take off," I said, stepping back.

"No—come on," he insisted. "I told my parents what
you did for me, saving my violin and all, and I know they'd
like to thank you. Besides, you'd be doing me and Marcy a
favor. I mean, there's all these old people in there, and it's
really boring once we stop playing."

I started to say no, but there was something about
his crooked grin and the look in his eyes; I knew that I
couldn't turn him down again, and it didn't take an idiot to
see he wanted to be my friend. And I guess I finally realized
that the lasting ache in my gut had less to do with being
hungry and more to do with being lonely.

"You sure it'll be all right? I mean, I'm not dressed
right or anything."

"Absolutely," Elvis said, his smile widening as he held
open the door for me to come inside.

I glanced over my shoulder, out across the dark lawn
and the lake beyond. "What the hell," I muttered under my
breath as I stepped into another world. Classical music was
now playing softly over the speakers, and the tempting
smell of great food drifted in the air. Everything seemed to
glitter and sparkle like it was sprinkled with diamond dust.

Marcy pushed her hair out of her eyes and waved shyly at me; there was even a sparkle about *her* that I'd never noticed before.

I was suddenly aware of how I looked compared to everyone else: I had on a ratty old sweatshirt and jeans, which went perfectly with my beat-up running shoes. What was I thinking, going in there? I didn't look that much better than Sir Lionel, and I wondered if I smelled as bad—not just my shoes. I fought back a powerful urge to sniff my armpit.

But Marcy didn't seem to care. She was smiling at me anyway.

"You look—I mean, you were great," I said.

"You're just saying that," she said, her face flushing.

"No, he isn't," Elvis said. "At least, I hope he isn't. And you do look quite fine, if I do say so myself," he added.

"Shut up," Marcy growled, "or I'll hurt you."

"Really, you were great. I heard the music from the path by the lake, and I just couldn't stay away."

"Thank you," Marcy said, then frowned at Elvis.

"Yeah, it means a lot, coming from you," Elvis added.

Now it was my turn to frown. "No problem. You guys are great. You don't really need me to tell you that, do you?"

Elvis laughed. "I guess not, but it's nice to hear anyway, particularly since you never say much, if anything."

I was about to argue the point, but the look on his face made me hesitate. Besides, he had a point. "Guilty as charged," I said.

I noticed that Marcy's hands were twisting and her face was so red, she looked like she was about to explode. "What is it, M?" Elvis asked.

"Well, Jace Adams," she said, glaring at me, "I'm just mad at you, that's all."

Elvis rolled his eyes. "Before you get into that, why don't we get something to eat?" he suggested.

I glanced at Marcy, wondering if it might be better if I headed in the opposite direction. I remembered the snide little comments she made that first day in orchestra class— not even close to friendly. But I was hungry, and the food won out. So I followed them to the buffet, where the crowd had thinned out. There was plenty left, but I didn't recognize hardly any of it.

"What's that?" I asked, pointing at a bowl of oatmeal-colored mush with a shudder.

"Dragon snot," Elvis said, stifling a chuckle, "with garlic and capers."

"Oh, that makes all the difference," I said, jabbing my finger into the mix, ignoring a gasp of horror from the poodle-haired woman on the other side of the buffet table. Defiant, I stuck my finger in my mouth and grinned at her.

"Ick," Marcy said. "Now nobody can eat it—boy germs."

"Wow," I murmured. And I wasn't faking it; it really tasted great. I reached for another sample, but Marcy intercepted my hand, guiding it to some chunks of bread next to it.

"It's called *hummus*. And it's even better with pita bread," Marcy said. "And if you use the bread instead of your fingers, you won't gross everyone out."

"So what's the deal? What's this party about, anyway?" I asked, spooning hummus onto my plate and grabbing a fistful of pita bread. I gave Marcy a wary glance.

"Anniversary," Elvis said proudly. "My parents—married thirty years."

Living with someone for that long? That's cool. I almost said so, but for once, I did the smart thing and kept quiet. Elvis led the way towards a happy-looking couple at the end of a long table. The man looked like an older version of Elvis, but without the red Afro. He looked up and stared at me, a puzzled look on his face. I was sure I stood out—and not only because I was dressed like a slob. But as I checked out the rest of the crowd, I saw a fair number of African Americans and Asians, so it wasn't the color of my skin he was staring at.

"Mom, Dad," Elvis announced, "this is Jace—the guy I told you about from school. You know, the one who helped me out—with the violin."

Elvis's dad almost knocked his chair over as he jumped up. I held out my hand and braced myself, but he grabbed me in a huge bear hug, slapping me on the back. "Well, well, Jace, I'm very glad to meet you," Mr. Goldberg said. "And I want to thank you for stepping in and helping Elvis. We owe you so much for that."

I mumbled something in response and didn't dare 'fess up that I couldn't have cared less what happened to Elvis; it was all about the violin. I got a hug from Elvis's mother, too, who gently touched my right cheek in gratitude. She had close-cropped hair, smooth skin, and clear gray eyes, and I liked her immediately.

"Jace, what a pleasure to meet you," Mrs. Goldberg said. "Elvis says you're a wonderful cellist."

I shrugged. "He and Marcy are the real musicians."

"Don't say that," Marcy said, her hands clenched. "Just don't."

Elvis's mom gave Marcy a questioning look.

"You should have heard him," Marcy said. "He was playing outside of Benaroya Hall. He was—" She shook her head and looked down, unable to finish. Her dark hair, streaked with green this time, hid her face. There was an awkward moment of silence.

"Maybe I should go," I mumbled. I was completely confused. *Does Marcy hate me that much?* I guessed she did.

"Absolutely not," Elvis's dad said. He grabbed me by the shoulder and walked me back over to the table piled with food. "There's plenty to eat here, so help yourself. Marcy's blood sugar is probably just low; I'm sure she didn't mean anything."

I didn't think her blood sugar had anything to do with it, but who was I to argue? I noticed that Elvis had led Marcy over to a corner of the room and was talking to her. She was shaking her head, her face pale. I filled my plate without paying attention to them; as soon as I was done eating, I'd go. Coming inside had been a mistake; I knew that now. For consolation, I started chomping on a piece of celery. I didn't notice Elvis standing beside me until he started talking.

"Come on," he said, grabbing my plate and pushing me towards a table where Marcy was now sitting. "Sit down," he ordered. "It's time to clear the air."

I flopped into a chair and pointed at my plate. "Help yourself. I'm not hungry anymore." Marcy grabbed a carrot, dipped it into some ranch dressing, and bit off the end.

Elvis tapped the tabletop in front of Marcy. "Okay, so talk," he ordered.

Marcy took another bite, then glanced up at Elvis, then me. I almost flinched. Her eyes showed so much pain.

"You," she said, her voice soft.

"Me? What did I do?"

"Typical guy," she snorted. "Completely clueless. Let's see if I have it right. You hop from school to school, never make any friends, never let anyone touch you, and, as a result, never realize what you miss and leave behind."

I popped a black olive into my mouth and sucked on it, taking that moment before I said anything. I looked at Elvis for support, but he stayed silent. He wasn't smiling anymore.

"We all heard you in class," Marcy continued. "And okay, I was bitchy to you that first day. And I heard you that night on the street—jeez. You have no idea how good you are, do you? Or maybe you do, and you're just an arrogant prick. My dad . . . " She spit out the words. "My dad heard you that night, too. He said you were a marvel—a marvel!" Her voice trailed off. She looked miserable.

My head was spinning; it was hard to sort out what she was saying. Somehow, I'd done something wrong by trying to be a good cellist. But I knew I hadn't done anything wrong, so I was completely confused. *She hates me? She likes me?* It was time to give up.

"Maybe I should go," I said. Before I had a chance to move, Elvis grabbed my arm. But this time, I shook it off, and he raised both hands in the air.

"C'mon. Don't run off. She's a little nuts, but she's not mad at you. Are you, Marcy?"

Marcy looked up at me and shook her head no.

"In fact, I think she actually likes you," Elvis said.

Marcy jabbed him in the ribs. "I'm sorry," Marcy said, her voice stronger as she glared at Elvis. "It's so stupid. I'm so stupid." She twisted a strand of her hair, not looking at me. "See, it's my dad. I know how this'll sound kinda lame, but he doesn't give a crap what I do—never has. It's not worth explaining why, and you probably wouldn't care anyway. But there's one exception, and that's when I'm playing the cello. That's when he actually sees *me*, not the son he never had or my stupid older sister—" Her voice trailed off, and I wasn't sure I understood what was going on or how I was part of it.

"But Marcy, you're really good," I said.

"Shut up," she snapped. "You're better. I mean, I'm not even in the same league as you. And now all he can talk about is how great you are. He's bugging me about who you're taking lessons from and when you'll be doing a recital. And I can't tell him that you're playing last chair in the orchestra; it's so unfair of Mr. Whitehead to keep you there, and we all know it, and I feel like it's my fault, and I—I—"

I had to admire her toughness; her chin trembled, but no tears. And man, I'd gotten it all wrong. All this time, I'd thought she was stuck up or something, but the exact opposite was true. She'd been upset by how her dad was treating *her* and how Mr. Whitehead was treating *me*. I was stunned. Except for Derrick, I couldn't remember the last time anybody actually cared much about what happened to me.

I pushed my plate in her direction. "I think you should have another carrot," I said. She wiped her nose and giggled, and then we were all laughing.

"I'm sorry about your dad," I said, reaching out to touch Marcy's hand—and then stopping myself. She noticed, and her face turned red.

"He may be a shitty father," Marcy said hurriedly, "but he does know a thing or two about music and musicians. And you're really good, you know. Are you studying with anyone?"

I shook my head. "I've taken lessons before, but I didn't know how long we were going to be here, so—" I didn't tell them about my plans to move back to California, but I think they got the idea.

"Well, Elvis had a thought," she said, looking at him.

"Have you ever heard of the Volt competition?" he asked.

I shook my head no.

"Well, it's the national competition for minority string players in high school," Elvis said. "The best African-American and Latino musicians try out for it, and this year, it's in Seattle—in February, to be exact. We think you should go for it."

"Yeah," Marcy said, her eyes bright.

I popped another olive into my mouth and sat back and listened as Marcy and Elvis told me more about the Volt competition, the tryouts, and the entry fee. It was clear that they'd been thinking about this for a while. Or maybe a better word would be *scheming*. But I had no interest in playing in some snooty competition. After all, Mom and I'd be leaving for some new city soon, and once that happened, no way could I find the money to enter or get her permission to come back for this Volt thing.

"All of the finalists get some awesome prizes, too," Elvis said.

I sat up straight. "Prizes?"

Marcy nodded.

"Like what?" I asked.

Elvis looked at Marcy. "Music scholarships," she said. She must have seen the look on my face. "What, you aren't planning to go to college?"

"Let's just say that's about as likely as me landing on Mars."

Elvis laughed. "Don't sell yourself short," he said. "There are some cash awards, too," he added. "First prize is a scholarship *and* $10,000."

Now it was my turn to grab a carrot stick and start chomping. "Okay. Now you got my attention."

By the time they'd run through all the details, we'd filled up our plates a couple more times. Marcy and Elvis even invited me to join their duo. "We'll make more money as a trio," Elvis said. For gigs like this, we're getting $300. And every few weeks, we play on the ferry between Seattle and Bainbridge Island. Captive audience, too. Mostly attorneys and old people. You'd be surprised how well we do. Interested?"

"Sh—sure," I stuttered. And then, in a flash, I wondered if I was being punked. I couldn't help it; I mean, what did I have in common with these two? Absolutely nothing. And if it wasn't a setup of some kind, maybe it was just pity, me being the poor black kid and them feeling sorry for me; I hated that idea more than anything.

"Why are you doing all this? I asked coldly. There weren't many answers I would've accepted. I mean, if Elvis or Marcy didn't say the right thing, I was going to flip over the table and tell them they could take their little group and stick it somewhere. But if Elvis noticed a change in my attitude, he didn't give it away.

"We're all strings, man," he said, "and strings gotta stick together." Marcy and Elvis gave each other a high five. "Plus, we figure a little diversity wouldn't hurt the take," he said.

His response was just stupid enough to be true. We *were* members of the same gang—the gang of strings. And I could handle being the token black dude if it meant more money.

"Now it comes out," I said with a grin. "You just want to use me. I feel so—cheap."

"Feels good, doesn't it?" Marcy said with a laugh. "Welcome to the club."

11

On Monday, I ate lunch with Marcy and Elvis. I could see a few other kids around the cafeteria staring at me, puzzled. After my first day at school, I'd done a decent job of disappearing into the background, so they probably were wondering who the new kid was. For once, I didn't mind the scrutiny.

As I ate a greasy burrito, Elvis slid a piece of paper with a list of names on it across the table. "Some cello teachers—suggestions from my teacher," he said. "I told him about you. No sweat if you don't like any of them, but if you're going for the Volt, you'll need the help of a real pro."

I finished my burrito and licked my fingers; I was still hungry. I had a cheese stick left, a pickle, and a bag of potato chips. It wasn't what you'd call a healthy organic meal for a kid who's still growing. I glanced at Elvis's lunch: two baloney sandwiches with cheese, lettuce, and tomato; a ripe red apple; some cheese and crackers; and a PowerBar for later.

"You aren't looking at the list," he said.

I licked my lips. "Sorry, I'm a little distracted."

"You want one of my sandwiches?" he sighed.

"Nah. That's okay," I said halfheartedly.

"Come on, I got a spare. And I'm not all that hungry, anyway. My mom always wants me to have extra food 'cause I'm so scrawny."

"Really, I don't want to take away your food."

"Don't be such a baby, Jace," Marcy said. "Just take it, before you start drooling."

"You'd be doing me a favor," Elvis lied. "I'd just throw it away. See, I'll just toss it in the trash right now." He grabbed a sandwich and wound up for a toss.

"Well—" I said.

"Suit yourself." He cocked his arm, but before he had a chance to throw, I snatched it from him.

"Thanks," I said.

"Don't mention it."

I opened the bag, pulled out the sandwich, and took a big bite. It tasted as good as it looked, thick with mayonnaise. "My compliments to your mom," I said between bites.

"I make my own lunch," Elvis replied.

"Well, maestro, you get my compliments, then. Can I get some relish on my sandwich tomorrow?"

"No way," Elvis complained. "Tomorrow, you mooch from Marcy."

We all laughed.

As I took another bite, I scanned the list of music teachers. I stopped at one name. Majykowski? Where had I seen that name before? And then I remembered—the business card with the hundred-dollar bill.

"What do you know about this guy?" I asked, tapping the name.

Elvis bit into his apple, leaned forward, and stared at the paper. "Majykowski?" He made a face as he said it. "Oh, yeah. Well, I probably wouldn't bother with him."

"Why not?"

"I mean, he's great and all. Or he was, anyway. He's foreign, probably from Europe, anyway—and old. He survived the Commies. He was supposed to be some sort of cello genius, until he pissed off the secret police by leading anti-government demonstrations. They broke his hands to teach him a lesson."

"Are you kidding me?"

Elvis shook his head. "He could never play again. So he came here and was a music professor at the University of Washington for a long time. A lot of really great cellists trained with him. But I heard he's a little nuts. He quit working, married some poet or painter or something. I guess it took him that long to find someone who'd put up with him."

"And how does all of that make him nuts?" Marcy said. "It sounds to me like he's got guts."

Elvis's face darkened. "He's a jerk," he said. "My mom sent me to one of his weekend workshops when I was younger. When we made a mistake or didn't pay attention, he screamed at us."

Now it was my turn. "And?" I said.

"I didn't like him," Elvis whined. "Besides, I was only seven."

"And?" Marcy and I both said it in unison.

Elvis's face reddened. "I started crying when he yelled at me, and then he sent me out of the room. How do you think that made me feel?"

"You poor baby," Marcy cooed. "You never had a mean teacher before that?"

"That's not the point," Elvis protested. He bit savagely into his remaining sandwich. "He didn't need to yell like that. Why are you asking about him, anyway?"

I thought for a moment; I knew Elvis was trying to change the subject. And since friends were still a new thing for me, the whole idea of confiding in them and telling them embarrassing stuff that'd happened, well, it was all very strange. I took a deep breath and decided to go for it.

"You know that night when I played on the street and you saw me?" I gestured towards Marcy.

She nodded. Elvis quit chewing and waited for me to go on.

"Well, I made some decent money that night," I continued. "In fact, somebody tossed a hundred-dollar bill into my case."

"I just bet it was my father," Marcy exclaimed, her eyes flashing anger now.

"No, it wasn't him. There was a business card paper-clipped to the money, and the name on the card was Majykowski. He wrote a note on the back, too."

"Did he think you were cute and wanted you to call him?" Elvis snickered.

Marcy slapped Elvis's shoulder. "Will you let him finish?"

"I don't remember what he wrote." But that was a lie. He said to call him if I wanted to make a difference or change the world or something like that. *What a joke.*

"So do you still have his card?" Elvis asked, dragging out the words.

"Maybe," I said.

"I wonder where he lives," Marcy said.

"Bainbridge Island," I replied. It sounded kinda cool—living on an island and all.

"Bainbridge Island's beautiful," Marcy remarked. "It's a half-hour ferry ride from downtown. But I think you should call him. And then, if it sounds legit, maybe we could go meet him?"

She smiled at me, and I got the distinct impression that her use of *we* didn't include Elvis. If I wasn't careful, I was going to start liking Marcy. Elvis looked at Marcy and then at me. He shook his head and bit into his sandwich.

"You two are trouble," he muttered.

12

The following Friday afternoon, I had my first cross-country meet. I'd decided after the first two practices that I hated running. I guess if I wasn't so scared of Bernice, I'd have quit and dealt with the consequences. But I didn't want to end up like one of her ex-husbands—like, dead and buried in her backyard. So I stuck with it, even though running was a lot harder than any other sport I'd tried and way more work than surfing. When you run, you have to decide how much pain you can stand; if you can put up with more of it than the other guy, you have a pretty good chance of beating him—it's just how running works. But by the end of the first week of cross-country, I found out that I actually *didn't* hate running. Sure, I had to run until I felt like I was going to barf, and then I ran some more. But when we were done, I felt really good, kind of like how I felt when I was playing the cello.

By the end of my second week of practice, I was strong enough to keep up with most of the JV guys. We'd work out by running around Green Lake one day, then do hills the next, and then go around the golf course the day after.

We did loop runs of five and six miles, but we also trained for shorter distances, like just a lap around the track. But here's where it would get stupid: we'd do twelve laps in a row, all at three-quarter speed, and with only a twenty-second break between laps. It was crazy. After about five laps, my body would start screaming. It was, like, I couldn't run another step. But guess what? My body's a frickin' liar, 'cause I could still go another couple of miles. Knowing this didn't make it any easier, but at least it gave me something to bad-mouth—when I wasn't gasping for breath.

On the day of my first race, I was really nervous, even though the course was only five kilometers—that's about 3.2 miles. I'd invited Mom to come watch, but I wasn't really expecting her to show up. She said she'd try, but I'd heard that a thousand times before; she hardly ever made it to anything. And even though Bernice would be driving her bus at starting time, I'd told *her* about the meet, too. But I wasn't exactly counting on her to show, either.

Just before starting time, all the runners crowded up to the starting line. I wasn't good enough to be near the front, but that was okay; neither was Elvis. Yeah, that's right—he was a runner, too. Another thing we had in common. And as we stood waiting side by side, he slapped me on the butt and told me to go for it. I gave him a look—and then slapped his butt back. Stupid, I know, but you can get away with butt slapping if you're in one of the more traditional sports. Just don't try it with skaters or surfers. And seriously, don't ever try it with a girl; it's not worth the world of trouble it'll bring.

As we waited for the starting gun to go off, I switched my watch to timer mode, taking deep breaths and exchanging nervous glances with a few other teammates. I still didn't know all of their names, but they nodded at me and smiled, so I nodded back. I knew I'd do my best to beat them—and Elvis, too. He wasn't getting any slack from me.

At the starter's gun, we all took off. By the first turn, I'd already settled into a comfortable pace, elbowing guys who crowded me. The course was a 2.5-kilometer loop, and we'd run the loop twice. It was mostly flat, except for a big hill in the middle that was a gut-busting grind on the way up and a wild, flailing dash back down.

Coach Ford stood near the edge of the course, about a half mile beyond the starting line. He was wearing navy blue nylon sweats and an old L.A. Lakers basketball cap instead of his usual suit and tie. He yelled something at me about being in second place as I ran past him, chanting out my time. I didn't get it; I could see at least half a dozen runners ahead of me. But then I realized what he meant: there was only one JV runner ahead of me. I was now the second fastest runner on the JV team. I was so stunned that I actually slowed to a trot, but not for long.

On the second lap, as I was going up that blasted hill for the second time, my legs screamed, my lungs burned, and I felt like someone had tied a belt tightly around my chest, making it hard to breathe. That's when I saw Marcy watching from halfway up the hill. She yelled something as I struggled past her, but I couldn't make out the words over the sound of my thundering heart and the blood rushing in my ears.

At the top of the hill, I almost slowed for a second time—because there was Bernice in her uniform, watching and smiling in a sad sort of way. She pumped her fist, nodded, and whooped as I went by, cheering me on in her own loud, scary way. Just seeing her there gave me a sudden surge of energy; *Bernice had actually taken the time to show up to my meet!*

It got easier after that; the course was downhill, so I let gravity pull me along as my stride got longer and my legs moved faster, even though they felt like they'd fall off. But then, as I made the final turn, with just 200 yards left to the finish line, a runner with flying red hair pulled up beside me—Elvis. His mouth was hanging open, and his arms were like windmills as he pumped them with effort. As we raced side by side down the last stretch, I had to fight back laughter. Who'd have guessed I'd be racing against my friend as we pounded across the finish line?

Elvis ended up beating me by a nose when he leaned ahead of me at the very end. Even though I called him a bastard, I didn't really care that he won. If somebody had to beat me, I was glad it turned out to be Elvis. His mom and dad were there, and they waved at me. Then they came up and slapped Elvis on the back in congratulations as he leaned over, hands on his knees, trying to suck in some air.

I stood there with my hands on my waist, breathing heavily. I felt terrible, but I also felt great. I looked around for Bernice but didn't see her. I didn't see my mom either— what a surprise. Just once, it'd be nice if she'd surprise me in a good way for a change.

"Good job, Stringz," Marcy said as she walked up behind me. "I think it's a good nickname, don't you?" She surprised me with a slap on the butt and then stepped away before I had a chance to give her one back. I was still out of breath, so all I could do was nod. "I think the name fits. You know, you play a string instrument," she explained, "and you're kinda built like a string—not much meat on your bones or your scrawny butt." She flicked her hair out of her eyes and smiled.

"Okay, okay," I protested. "Enough about my scrawny butt, and no more slapping. Otherwise, I might have to turn you in for sexual harassment or something. And if I'm going to be *Stringz*, that just means I get to come up with a nickname for you, too."

Marcy's eyes narrowed. "But only if it's nice."

"How 'bout *Butt-Slapper*?"

"No way."

I didn't get a chance to make any other suggestions— not that she was getting a vote on it, anyway—because Elvis staggered up and wrapped his arms around me like we were long-lost brothers or something. For a moment, I couldn't figure out what to do, but then I just gave up and hugged him back.

"Nice race, man," he said. "Wow, you were flying on that first lap. I didn't think I was gonna be able to catch you. Coach said if we keep this up, the guys on the varsity squad'll be in trouble."

"I don't know about that," I said, "but you ran a good race—showed a lot of grit, you know?"

He shrugged. "Another week or two of practice, and

there's no way I'd be able to catch you. So it was now or never."

I didn't believe him, but it was nice to hear him say it anyway.

"Did you call that Magic guy yet?" Marcy asked.

"You mean Mr. Majykowski?"

"Yeah, him," she said.

I gave her a sheepish look. "Can't it wait until tonight?" I said.

"Um, no," Marcy said, her eyes narrowing.

"Gimme a break. I just ran my guts out. There're probably bits and pieces of my lungs scattered all over the course."

"Oh, you mean the race you just *lost*?" She smiled at me as she said that.

"No, I mean the race that I finished incredibly well for someone who's just gone out for cross-country," I retorted. But I could tell she wasn't paying any attention to what I'd said; instead, she turned away, pulled out her cell phone, punched in a number, and then handed it to me.

I backed away as if she'd handed me something with fangs. "What are you doing?"

"Come on, don't be such a baby," she said. "Take it."

"Why should I?"

Marcy gave me a smug little smile. "Because I just made the call for you. And you're going to feel like an idiot when he answers the phone. I figure now's a great time to start working on my project to turn you into a kind of American Idol for classical, geeky guys."

I felt like flinging the phone across the field; I wasn't

ready for lessons or any kind of plan B, C, or X. But Marcy was staring at me, her face half covered by her bangs and her dark eyes glittering. This was a test I probably didn't want to fail.

I heard a faint voice from the phone: "Hallo, hallo?"

"All right," I hissed, then grabbed the phone and jammed it up to my ear. "Yes, yes, hello," I said quickly. "Is Mr. Majykowski there?"

Marcy mouthed the word *please*.

"Please," I added.

"Who is this?"

"Jace Adams," I said.

"I know no Jace Adams," said the voice on the other end of the line. "What are you trying to sell me?"

"I don't want to sell you anything. You asked me to call you. I mean, Mr. Majykowski asked me to call him. I mean, he wrote it on his business card and—"

"What?" I could tell the voice was just seconds away from hanging up on me.

"You see, I play cello and . . . "

"Ahh! You are the young man who was playing the cello on the sidewalk, yes?" the voice interrupted.

"Yeah, I guess that's right."

"You are either the young man I heard playing cello weeks ago on the street who I invited to call me but who has neglected to do so for such a long time that I am tempted to call him rude, or you aren't. Which is it?"

I stood there for a few seconds with my mouth half open. "If you mean," I finally managed to say, "the kid who was playing outside of Benaroya Hall about a month ago, then yeah, that's me. Somebody dropped a card clipped to a hundred-dollar bill that had your name on it, so I figured it was you."

"The money was my wife's idea." I could hear him laughing. "She said that if I wanted to land a fish, I needed to bait the hook. And I see that she was right."

"I'm not sure you landed me yet, but we're talking," I said.

"Well, I am Majykowski. I am a music teacher. Cello is my passion. Is it yours?"

"Um, I don't know," I replied. I wasn't used to anyone being so direct.

"Honest answer. That is something. Are you taking private lessons now?"

"No."

"Would you like to?"

I was definitely interested; I hadn't had any time to think about it yet, but there was something about this guy I liked. There was no bullshit going on. "Maybe," I said. I wasn't going all in—at least, not yet.

"You come out here, and I hear you play again. Then we talk. And then you decide. What do you think?"

"How much?" I asked.

Now he was laughing, so loud that I had to take the phone away from my ear.

"How much you have?" Majykowski said.

"I might still have your hundred-dollar bill," I said.

More laughter. "That's good. You come tomorrow, and we talk about it then. Saturday at noon."

I started to reply but heard a good-bye and the phone went dead.

Elvis was already leaving, and he waved in my direction. "You can tell me about the call tomorrow," he yelled, then headed to the parking lot with his parents on either side of him, their arms draped affectionately over his shoulders. *Bastard,* I thought as I watched them leave. And this time I meant it. I'd have given just about anything for my mom to show up at the meet. I turned away for a second and swiped at my eyes with the back of my sleeve. I was careful not to look directly at Marcy.

"Well?" Marcy held out her hand for her phone. "What's the deal?"

"Uh, yeah, I guess I have an appointment with him at noon tomorrow."

When Marcy didn't say anything, I looked at her. She was staring at me and biting her lip. "You okay?" she asked.

"Yeah, sure," I replied, more harshly than I intended. "Just great."

"So you think he'll mind if I go with you? We can play as we take the ferry. I could use some extra cash. And then we hop off, go visit this character, and then play on the way back. It'll be perfect."

Before I could say anything, we heard a honk from the parking lot. "There's my ride," Marcy said. "So it's all set. I'll meet you tomorrow at the ferry terminal, Colman Dock, eleven o'clock sharp." Then she turned and trotted off to the car without waiting for a word from me. I watched her slip inside, talking animatedly to the woman driving—her mom—who was smiling and nodding.

I wondered if she and Elvis realized how lucky they were to have parents like theirs. Probably not.

13

As I trudged up the walk to Bernice's house, I was surprised to see her sitting on the porch, cigarette smoke drifting out over the lawn.

"Nice race," she said.

"What?"

"I'd expect your *legs* to be tired after that race, but not your ears."

"Oh . . . um, thanks." It was the first time Bernice had ever said something positive to me, and I wasn't used to it.

"You need to sit, and we need to have a little chat."

Another chat. Oh, crap. I dropped my backpack and the cello case on the porch, then settled into the worn wicker chair and waited while Bernice smoked.

"This used to be a nice neighborhood," she said finally. "It's all too fixed up now. People working at Microsoft and all those other high-tech places keep moving in, fancying up their houses, making my taxes go up and all."

"You have a nice house, too," I said blandly.

"My first husband was good for something. He said Green Lake would be a good place to own real estate. He was right. Made him mad when I got the house in the divorce, but I knew he was right. Husbands two and three helped me pay off the mortgage. So now, it's just taxes, and that's it. I figure to stay here till I die."

"Sounds good," I said.

She looked sharply at me.

"I don't mean the dying part," I added quickly. "I meant about staying here."

She nodded and sucked on her cigarette. I started tapping my foot, figuring a chat about real estate wasn't what was really on her mind.

"Thanks for coming to my race," I said, tired of waiting for her to get to the point. "I appreciate it. I don't suppose you happened to see Mom there?"

Bernice sighed. "Your momma's gone. She left town this morning."

And just like that, the bottom dropped out of my life. I grabbed the armrests of the wicker chair and held on. I'd been hoping Mom would surprise me someday, but not like this. Just goes to show that you gotta be careful what you wish for.

Bernice let her words simmer for a bit, then she continued. "Not sure you knew about it, but she found a man at that place where she was working." She shook her head.

Now all that working late suddenly made sense. How could I have been so stupid? I took off my glasses, rubbed my eyes, and then put the glasses back on.

"She left town?" I asked, mostly to myself, still trying to get my head around it.

"He got transferred to Denver," she continued. "Asked her to go with him."

I wiped my eyes again. "What do you mean?" I asked. My voice was shaking; it sounded like someone else was talking—even to me.

"Her boyfriend—I think she called him Leon—wasn't interested in her having any—well, *baggage*. That's the word he used."

"Baggage?" I sputtered.

Bernice nodded, her lips narrowing. "So your mother and I had a talk a few nights ago. She's no lovesick teenager anymore. She's a grown-up woman—with not just one child, but two."

I blinked. I imagined I could hear someone screaming, and it seemed to come from far away. "Baggage?" I repeated. I was still stuck on that word.

"I'm not one to sugarcoat," Bernice said. "It's not my nature. Even though I never had my own babies, I know what is right and what isn't. I told her she was going to have to make a choice. Wouldn't be fair to you, otherwise."

"What do you mean?" Considering the bomb she had just dropped on me, I was surprised I could still talk.

Bernice sucked on her cigarette, and the end glowed red. "I told her I didn't want her running all over the world with some yahoo, treating you like—"

"Baggage," I finished for her.

She nodded.

"Eventually, she agreed with me." Bernice was rubbing her hands together, and I wondered if she'd ever used them on my mom. *A slap from Bernice would hurt.* "She'd been planning to send you away, to some military school or something. But I got her to see that maybe it was time you got settled in a place for more than a few months and had a chance to make some friends."

"I have friends in California," I said, the lie coming easily.

Bernice shrugged. "But you ain't there anymore. 'Course, all this is up to you. You can stay here with me, or else you can go to that military school back east that your momma picked out for you—a place for kids who have a talent with guns instead of musical instruments, I guess. That wouldn't be such a bad choice."

The screaming in my mind was getting louder, and it was hard to think. *Baggage?* That's what he thought of me? He never even met me! But Mom had made her choice: she was doing what he wanted, not what *I* wanted—not that anyone had asked me. And that made me wonder if that's what I'd been all along to her: *nothing more than baggage.*

Bernice's voice softened. "I know I'm not the easiest person to be around. I got three ex-husbands to vouch for that. But I just want you to know that I think you're all right—for a teenage boy, that is."

"Coulda fooled me," I said. At that point, I really didn't care what she thought.

"Well, like I said, I'm not a nice person. But I'll say this and mean it: I'd be more 'n proud to have you stay here with me.

I took a shaky breath. "What choice do I have?" I said.

Bernice shrugged. "The way I see it, you got two choices: one from your momma, and I'm giving you another one. You don't have to take it."

My head was spinning. "I don't know what to say."

This news changed everything and nothing. If I stayed, I could still leave whenever I wanted; I just wouldn't be living with Mom. Even if Bernice knew about my third option, it didn't sound like she'd do anything to stop me. And then I'd be on my own for sure.

"No hurry from me," Bernice said. "Take as much time deciding as you want. And if you want, in the meantime you can move inside."

I didn't need to think too long about her offer. "Thanks," I said.

"No problem," Bernice said with a shrug. "And just so it's clear, I won't be forcing you to stay with me. Now, that doesn't mean I don't *want* you to stay or that it wouldn't be good for you; it just means that you and me, well, I'll be treating you like a man, not a boy. Understand?"

"She just left without saying anything, without even leaving me a note or a message or anything?" I had to be sure.

Bernice took another long pull on her cigarette, looked in my eyes, and just sighed. And that was answer enough.

"What did I ever do to her?" I whispered.

"Nothing," Bernice said, her dark eyes flaring with sudden anger. "It ain't your fault. And I'll kick your ass if you act like it was. You hear me?" She said this with a surprising fierceness. "Your mom, she said she'd call sometime soon and explain everything to you once they get to Denver."

"I won't hold my breath."

"Now you're learnin'," Bernice replied with a snort.

I got up, went through the house and out to my castle. Once I closed the door, I wadded up a T-shirt over my mouth so nobody could hear me. I guess I wasn't as tough as I thought.

14

I woke up in the middle of the night, stumbled outside, and, out of habit, peed on Bernice's flowers. *Oh, crap*, I thought, when I realized what I was doing. None of this was Bernice's fault. She was as much a victim of my mom as I was. And playing mom to a teenager most likely wasn't part of her plans until now.

It was too bad Leon—or whatever his name was—hadn't left something behind. Then I could maybe take a bat to it. It was easy to imagine beating the hell out of his brand-new Mercedes or Lexus or BMW or whatever it was he drove that must have impressed my mother. And destroying it would feel great. I'd even pay money to do it—give the parking lot attendant my hundred-dollar bill and tell him to look the other way for a few minutes. "Don't mind the noise, dude," I'd say. "It's just me taking a little batting practice with my Louisville slugger."

Maybe a fire would be better, but a car'd be too dangerous to light up. And I wouldn't want anyone to think I was a pyromaniac. Or maybe Mom's new guy was a golfer; I still had fond memories of our sleazy apartment manager howling when he discovered what I'd done to his clubs. Served him right, too. Every time he'd see my mom, his eyes would bug out and he'd nearly trip over his tongue. And he had no right to talk to her the way he did just because I had no dad. But I took care of him.

It is what it is. Those words flickered across my mind, and I almost screamed with a sudden burst of rage and anger. *It didn't have to be this way.* It didn't. My mom could have stayed. She didn't have to ditch me. *She could have said no to him.*

I truly hated her for bringing me to Seattle, and I hated her more for leaving me behind.

Now, for the first time ever, I hated her as much as I hated my father. And I hated myself, too—for being such a fool. I wondered how long she'd been planning to ditch me. *How could I have missed it?*

The night was clear and cold. I shivered as I stood there in my sweatpants, staring at the stars. I felt so small—and alone. I went back inside and turned off my light, but I couldn't sleep. After tossing and turning for a while, I gave up. I turned on the light, took Ruby out, and played whatever came into my mind. I settled on the music of B.B. King, a famous old black musician who plays guitar and sings blues, that sad kind of music with roots in the songs my slave ancestors chanted in the cotton fields of the South. My baggage-free mom used to listen to him, and I always liked his stuff.

And so, in keeping with my crappy life, I started playing B.B.'s blues, singing along softly when I remembered the words. I didn't care if I woke up the neighbors; they could all rot in hell.

15

I was awake again before it was light outside. I rolled over, closed my eyes, and tried to fall back to sleep, but my brain was racing. My body was sore from the race, and that didn't help. But I also couldn't stop thinking about my mom. Maybe if I'd been a better son, she'd have stuck around instead of taking off with Leon.

And then I remembered: Marcy and I were going to be playing on the Bainbridge Island ferry in just a few hours, and I was meeting Mr. What's-his-name. I let out a loud groan; I still had time to cancel, but that would mean getting out of bed, going into the house and making phone calls, and maybe getting stuck talking to Marcy's mom or dad. It was way too much effort after so little sleep. I groaned again and pulled the pillow over my head. When I woke a few hours later, it was to the sound of someone banging on the door—Bernice.

"Hey, I made some coffee," she yelled. That was it. No "How you doing, Jace?" or "Can I bring you out some breakfast and then help you get moved inside?" On the other hand, Bernice hadn't ever come out to announce that

113

she'd made coffee, either, so maybe something really had changed.

As I threw on some clothes, a word began swirling through my mind: *Why? Why didn't Mom say something?* I mean, she could've come to me and said she had this great new boyfriend that she really loved—or at least liked a lot—but he was moving to Denver. Then she could've said she wanted to give the relationship a chance, so she was stuck on what to do: go with him, stay here, or what? Oh yeah, he wasn't into kids, so if she moved, I wouldn't be invited to go along with them.

Since I wasn't a complete jerk, I probably would've told her to go. Who was I to stand in her way? I wondered what a radio talk-show shrink might tell her. Maybe the shrink would stand up for me or remind her of her responsibilities. But maybe not. I mean, it wasn't like I was this great, amazing kid or anything. Maybe leaving was the right choice—for her. Maybe all the moving around, all the troubles she'd had over the years, maybe it was all because of me. Maybe she'd be better off without me, and this was her only way out.

It made me wonder if there was anyone else out there like me, going through this same pile of crap. If there was, I had only one thing I'd tell him: *Good luck, dude. You're gonna need it.* With that, I slipped out of the castle and up the back steps into the kitchen.

"You gonna be all right?" Bernice wasn't smoking this morning, and she looked at me over the rim of her coffee cup.

I shrugged. "I'll live. Just feeling a little, um—"

"Raw?" she suggested.

I shrugged again. "I'm not sure," I said. "Hollow, maybe. You can call me hollow dude—or something like that." I paused, then asked, "You think she's gonna be okay?"

Bernice thought for a moment, hiding the lower part of her face behind the coffee mug. I knew one thing: she wasn't one to sugarcoat anything. "Don't know, Jace. I may be mad at her, but I hope she'll be all right."

"I guess I'll be playing on the ferryboat today," I said. "I'll get my stuff moved into the bedroom before I go."

"Maybe you should just hang around here. I *might* even be nice to you." Bernice smiled.

And I had to smile back. "Probably better if I do something," I said. "That way I won't be alone, won't have time to sit around and think too much."

I saw Bernice's eyebrows jump. "But I didn't think you had any friends—yet."

"She's from the orchestra," I explained, feeling my face warm. "Her name is Marcy."

"Oh, I see." Bernice lit a cigarette. "You play for money?"

"Sure, why else would I be playing on a ferryboat? We play, and people chip in whatever they feel like."

"No kidding?" she said. I could see she was thinking about it. "Is it because you're that good or because they feel guilty?"

"You know when you called me lazy?" I asked.

"I do seem to remember something like that," Bernice replied, waving her cigarette in a slow arc over her head.

"Well, that night, I took a bus downtown and made over a hundred bucks playing on the sidewalk."

"So in other words, who cares if they're guilty white folks?"

"You got that right."

"Well, it's hard to argue with a hundred dollars," Bernice admitted. "But I wouldn't say that about making money some other, less appropriate ways, if you know what I mean. When will you be back home?"

That made me stop in my tracks; I hadn't thought about Bernice's house as home before that, but I guess Mom's taking off changed that, too. I shrugged. I could have kept quiet about my appointment with Mr. Majykowski, but I was tired of secrets.

"After dinner, I think. I'm also meeting a man who gives cello lessons."

"Where? On the ferry?"

"Nope, he lives on Bainbridge Island," I answered.

"How'd you hear about him?" Bernice asked.

"My friends," I said. "They asked their teachers."

Bernice nodded. "So now you got friends, plural?"

"Well," I stammered, "there's Marcy and this guy who plays the violin. His name is Elvis."

"Elvis?" Bernice mouthed, her eyebrows reaching skyward once again. "Are you kidding me?"

I shrugged and shook my head no.

Bernice shook her head, too. "Well then, have a good time. And thanks for telling me where you'll be."

"You'd worry?"

Bernice just sucked on her cigarette and laughed.

16

Soon, I was drinking McDonald's coffee and standing on the ferry terminal walkway at Colman Dock, staring in the direction of Bainbridge Island. It was a gorgeous day; the sky was deep blue, the waters of Elliott Bay sparkled, and the hills around the city were covered in orange, yellow, and red. It had to be a joke; I mean, how could the world look so great when my life was so shitty?

I guess I should have felt something. Anger, for sure. Betrayal? Ditto. But by the time I'd started sipping my coffee, I didn't feel anything at all; I guess I was just numb inside. I felt like Robotboy, and that was okay with me: the less I felt, the better. I took another sip of coffee and fought back a sudden urge to barf over the railing. My stomach felt like it was on fire, and coffee was adding fuel to the blaze. But I needed the coffee to help keep me awake, so nausea was one feeling I'd have to live with, robot or not.

Before too long I heard a whistle, and when I looked around for the source, I saw Marcy coming through the glass doors onto the walkway. She was smiling in a way that made her look cute in an artsy way. She wasn't the kind of girl who wore her clothes like flashing neon signs so that all you ever needed to know about her was right there, spelled out by what she was wearing. I was glad to see her, but my face must have showed something else, because her smile faded when she got closer.

"What's wrong?" she asked.

I shrugged. "I don't know. I feel a little queasy. Maybe a touch of flu or something."

"You want to cancel it?"

I appreciated the offer, but I could tell that she'd be disappointed if I said yes. And that's when I realized that I couldn't bear the thought of disappointing anyone else. I'd done that enough to my mom. I must have, or she wouldn't have left.

"Nah, I'm feeling better already," I said, forcing a smile. "I think a cruise is just what the doctor ordered."

Marcy eyed me warily. A horn blast announced the arrival of a Bainbridge Island ferry, its lower deck open and filled with cars lined up and out onto the bow. Above the main deck, I could see the passenger section, where people stood outside, enjoying the sunshine and fresh air. A plaque under the pilothouse displayed the ferry's name: *Wenatchee*.

We watched as it docked, and even before the ramp was lowered to let the cars off, the people who had walked on were already hurrying across the walkway from the main passenger deck into the terminal. We waited until the people swirling around us were all gone, and then it was our turn to board. I followed Marcy into the huge ferry cabin, which held miles of seats and narrow aisles. During the week, it was probably packed with people commuting to and from downtown Seattle. But on this Saturday morning, there were just a smattering of families and a few men who huddled over coffee, hid behind newspapers, or stared blankly out a window.

"Want some more coffee?" Marcy asked.

I touched my stomach and shook my head.

"Then follow me. It's pretty up on the sundeck. You can work on your tan." Marcy looked at me and smiled. When I didn't react, her smile faded. "Are you sure you're all right?"

I'd hoped that if I stayed quiet, she'd quit asking questions; I wasn't in the mood to be grilled, particularly by Marcy. I mean, it wasn't like she was my girlfriend or anything. We were barely even friends.

I glanced back. The walkway connecting the ferry's upper deck to the terminal was still in place; I could still change my mind. It'd serve her right for being so nosy if I just took off and left her alone on the boat. Marcy must have sensed what I was thinking and didn't give me a chance to run. Instead, she grabbed my hand and led me up the stairs.

"Thanks," I murmured, squeezing her hand back.

"What?" Marcy gave me a quizzical look. "Why are you acting so weird? Do you have brain damage from your race yesterday or something? I think we should forget playing for money and just enjoy the fresh air, okay?"

"Didn't you know?" I said.

"Know what?"

"That's my middle name. Jace *Weird* Adams."

"Oh, shut up," she said, smacking me in the chest.

"Here I was, trying to be nice, and you're making fun of me."

"Am not."

"Are too."

"Am not."

And that's how it went as I followed her up the stairs and out on the vast sundeck, which had groups of seats under a yellow Plexiglas ceiling. At either end of the ferry, a pilothouse jutted up above the deck. We found seats near the front of the ferry, though technically, there was no permanent front on a ferry like this one. The bow and stern were identical, and the ferry could load cars from either end without turning around. Front or back was just a matter of perspective.

We laid our cello cases on the deck, and Marcy took off her backpack. "I brought some food," she said.

"Good thinking."

Marcy set out cheese and crackers, four hard-boiled eggs, a couple of bananas, a sandwich bag full of nuts and raisins, two Milky Way bars, and a couple of napkins.

I realized I was starving as soon as I saw the food. My body didn't take a break just because it felt like the end of the world; I scarfed down two eggs and a banana, then stacked some cheese on the crackers and demolished it in one bite.

Marcy picked at a banana, eyeing me over the peel. I tried to ignore her, but it didn't work for long. "Okay, what is it?" I asked.

"You're giving it a good try," she said, "and it isn't like I know you all that well. But something's not right—I can tell. And I'm just wondering, well . . . you don't need to say anything about it. I mean, not if you don't want to. And it isn't like we're, you know, dating or anything. I just, well, I just hope that if I've done something wrong, you'll tell me and all. I don't have that many friends, and I don't know what I'd do if you just up and—I don't know—quit talking to me or looking at me the way you do sometimes—"

Her voice trailed off, and she broke off a piece of banana, then popped it in her mouth. She stared out over the water, and if I hadn't noticed the way she was holding her mouth, her lips were pursed like she was playing the oboe, or the way her right hand, the one holding the banana, was shaking slightly, I wouldn't have thought she gave a crap about me or anything else.

"What do you mean about the way I look at you?" I asked.

Marcy glanced at me with eyes so intent that I almost turned away. "Um, I guess it's a look like you cared," she said, tapping her lower lip with a finger.

"Oh" was all I could think to say.

I noticed an older couple watching us. I thought they'd frown or maybe look away, but the old guy just smiled at me and nodded, as if to say it'd be all right. The woman smiled, too. Then the old guy put his arm around his wife; I mean, I assumed it was his wife. Then he nodded again, and that's when I got it: he was demonstrating what he thought I should do. I really was such a moron.

I took a deep breath; the easy thing to do would be to get mad and ask her how this had become about her and me or, better yet, just pick up my stuff and find another place to sit. But I guess Marcy had noticed something I hadn't even realized myself: I did care about her. I *liked* her. *What the hell?* My arm felt like it weighed about a million pounds, but I carefully brought it over Marcy's shoulders and let it settle into place. I thought she'd jab me with an elbow or something, but she just blinked at me and then settled against me. I patted her back lightly, the way I might pat a dog or cat I didn't like that much.

"Does this mean you do care?" she asked. "You know, *friend* care, not, uh, anything else."

"Yeah," I said.

"Good," Marcy replied. "I do, too. And that's why I'm wondering what's going on."

I sighed. She was relentless. I guess that's one of the differences between guys and girls. I mean, we'll talk about sports or video games and tell fart jokes, but we never, ever talk about our feelings. I'm not sure if that's good or bad, but that's just how it works. So I was sitting there, thinking that if I told her about my mom, about what'd happened, it'd bring it all back. And that was the last thing I wanted to do. Or at least, that's what I thought.

But there must have been something about having Marcy right beside me like that, because something went "click" inside. And then I began to talk.

"My life is total crap, Marcy. That's why I'm acting weird." The words came out in a rush.

"So it's not me?"

"Are you serious?" I shook my head. "No, it's not you. You can relax your little self-absorbed head."

Marcy winced.

"I didn't mean it to come out like that," I said quickly. "You and Elvis are the, well, the best friends I've ever had. In fact, you're just about the *only* friends I've ever had."

"No way."

I nodded. "Way. That's one of the great things about always moving around. I've never had to bother with friends. We were never in one place long enough."

"Then what is it?"

I knew I had to tell it the way it was—no lying to make my mom sound better than she was, no lying to make me sound better than I was. So I told her everything: about moving all the time for years, about the stuff I'd done to my mom's boyfriends, about the stuff I'd done to the creepy guys who looked at my mom the wrong way, about never knowing who my dad was. And finally, I told her about my mom taking off to Denver with some loser named Leon. The only thing I *didn't* tell her was that I'd been sleeping in a shed. I still had some pride left. Marcy just sat there and listened; I didn't stop talking until the blast from the ferry's horn announced our arrival at Bainbridge Island.

"I don't know what to say," she whispered. "I had no idea. I'm really sorry, Jace."

"No reason for *you* to be sorry," I said quickly. "I mean, I'm not looking for pity or anything. Everyone has it rough from time to time, and I'm just—"

"Would you just shut up now?" Marcy interrupted. "Sure, you don't have cancer and somebody didn't just cut off your arm, but that doesn't make what you've had to go through okay."

"Alright, then," I laughed without any humor. "I suppose a little sympathy is good."

That's when she kissed me. I was so stunned, I forgot to kiss her back.

She leaned away with a faint smile on the edge of her mouth. "You don't need to worry, Stringz. Your secrets are safe with me. I won't tell anyone. And I'm glad you're making an exception to this stupid 'no friend' thing you've got going on."

I suppose if I was less of a complete dork, I could have said something perfectly cool at that point. Maybe even kissed her back. But instead, I just stammered, "Well, um, good. It's nice to have a friend; it's great to have friends. So remember, friend, to bring along some Twinkies next time."

"Twinkies?" Marcy exclaimed. "That's what I get? Twinkies?"

I thought she was going to slap me for sure. And I certainly deserved it. I mean, what a complete idiot. A hot girl just kissed me, and all I could do was blabber about junk food? I sat there for a while, looking stupid and confused. Just the sight of the dumb look on my face set her off. She doubled over, shrieking with laughter and gasping for air, tears streaming down her face. I watched her and then felt something break free inside of me, and I started laughing, too. We were making so much commotion that the seagulls on the railing gave us a strange look and flew away.

The old couple smiled at us, then left, hand in hand. Maybe I wasn't such a total loser after all.

17

Professor Majykowski said he lived just a ten-minute walk from the ferry terminal. I figured he must have one of the cool houses with views of the harbor I'd noticed from the ferry. But instead of turning right once we were outside the terminal, Marcy grabbed my hand again and pulled in the opposite direction.

"I hope you know where we're going," I mumbled.

She pulled her cell phone out of her pocket. "GPS," she replied.

I fought back a yawn; I was ready for a nap—or another ten cups of coffee. I sleepwalked next to Marcy, half listening as she filled me in on the history of the place. Not all that long ago, Bainbridge had been different; it was quieter and less connected to Seattle, more connected to the Sound and the forests and farms nearby. The people who lived there fished, logged, or farmed.

"Our family had a cabin, just over there," she said, pointing down a street crowded with tourist shops, towards a distant tree-covered hill. "We used to come here all the time when I was little. My grandfather was born here."

"What happened?"

"My grandparents died, and Dad sold the place. He said he needed the money for his business." I could hear the anger in her voice.

"Sounds like you're still pissed at them for dying—or at your dad for selling."

"It was Dad's fault," she said. "But that's just one among many things he's done that I hate."

If I could have felt anything, I might have been curious about what she meant, but I was back to feeling numb. I covered another yawn with my hand, and Marcy didn't seem to notice. Or maybe she did and figured that gabbing on would take my mind off my mom.

We followed Marcy's GPS directions. She turned at the end of the block, then headed down a steep hill. The road ended at a marina with a group of steel-sided buildings. And beyond that, I saw row after row of docks and slips, all but a few crowded with huge yachts. This was a place for rich people; you could almost smell it in the air. I wondered what these boats must cost. And I bet most just sat there in the water, gathering barnacles, waiting for the few weekends a year they were actually used. How could you have so much money that you could waste it like that? I didn't get it.

Marcy led me around the buildings, through the marina's gate, and then out on the docks. "We're looking for number 68," she reminded me.

We heard it before we saw it, because of the music echoing across the marina. Someone was listening to Beethoven the best way: LOUD. I motioned towards it, and we headed in that direction. The music was coming from a big white yacht that was tied up near the end of one of the docks. The boat looked about as long as a house trailer and nearly as wide, but it had a sharp, rakish bow. Its glass and chrome glistened in the sunshine, and a blue flag with a picture of a cello snapped in the breeze.

"This must be the place," I muttered.

"Professor Majykowski!" Marcy yelled. "Hello!"

"Mr. Majykowski? Anyone home?" I added.

The music stopped abruptly. "I just about gave up on you."

We looked up and saw a man with longish white hair and a thin, tanned face leaning out of a window. "Professor Majykowski?" we asked in unison.

"That was my name the last time I checked," he said, with a flourish of his hand.

"Permission to come aboard, sir?" I said formally, recalling people saying this in a movie.

Majykowski's eyes narrowed. "You must be Jace."

"Yessir."

"And you are a smarty pants?"

"I think you mean *punk*," I said, failing to hide a grin.

"And the answer is sometimes," Marcy finished for me. Then she made a face at me.

"At least *she* is honest," he grumped. "Permission granted for boarding. But first, who is this friend of Mr. Smart-Ass?"

"This is Marcy. She and I play cello in our school orchestra."

"Hmmm. Well, I guess she can do no harm. Both of

you, come aboard." He disappeared back inside. There was a ramp near the boat's stern, which Marcy and I used to cross. As we stepped onto the wooden deck, Majykowski met us in an open doorway that led inside to the boat's main cabin.

"Have you had your midday meal yet?" he asked.

"We had a snack on the ferry," Marcy replied.

"I will take that as a no," Majykowski said. "Well, come in. My wife is gone for a while, shopping. She despises Beethoven and loves shopping. We shall get acquainted meanwhile."

I followed Marcy down a short flight of steps, along a narrow hallway, and into what looked like a very cramped kitchen. There was room for only one person to sit in a chair, and Majykowski made it clear that he was it. He motioned towards a counter, and Marcy and I slid onto the chrome stools beside it.

"Nice kitchen," Marcy said.

"*Galley*, my dear, *galley*. That is the word we sailors use."

"Sorry," Marcy muttered.

Majykowski smiled. "I cook simple but good food," he said in a thick accent that made him sound a little bit like an older version of Arnold Schwarzenegger. "Tomato soup and grilled cheese sandwiches. Okey-dokey?"

Marcy nodded, but I looked at the professor with suspicion. How did he know that tomato soup and grilled cheese was one of my favorite meals? If I asked him about it, I'd sound like a nutball, so I kept my mouth shut. He poured the soup into bowls, put the sandwiches on plates, and slid them onto the counter across from us. By now, my mouth was watering. I hadn't realized I was still hungry.

"Good appetite," Majykowski said. We didn't need any further encouragement.

While we ate, Majykowski told us about himself: he was a retired professor and lived on the boat year-round with his wife and three cats, Fellini, Caruso, and Roberta (Bob for short). Except for the wife and the cats, it was all stuff Elvis had told me about him. I tried not to stare at his hands, but it was hard not to notice them. The fingers were twisted and swollen, and they pointed in several directions. Old white scars crisscrossed the backs of his hands, and I was surprised he could even use them, but he'd handled making lunch okay.

"I was done with teaching and the brats and all of it," he explained, "so I retired to spend time on my boat with my wife. So far, so good. And then one night a few months ago, I ran into my friend Sir Lionel, and in his own strange way, he tells me about this young man—Sir Lancelot is what he called you—who's playing cello on the streets."

I paused, cheese sandwich halfway to my open mouth. "You mean the homeless guy?"

"Actually, he prefers to be called *First Citizen of the City*," Majykowski corrected. "And yes, he and I are friends. Why is that so strange?"

"Oh, I don't know," I said in my best punk-ass voice, "maybe because you're rich and live on a yacht, whereas he's poorer than poor, wears rags, lives on a street corner, and everything he owns in the world fits in a shopping cart."

"I suppose one might look at it that way," Majykowski

said, raising his hand to interrupt. "Many people have tried to get Sir Lionel into a more permanent situation. I've even invited him to live with me, but he refuses, and I can't force him. He's as stubborn as he is talented."

"What do you mean, *talented*?" Marcy asked.

"He was one of my first students many years ago," Majykowski said. "He had a—how do you say it?—a breakdown." Majykowski shrugged. "His parents did what they could, but he refused treatment and then one day, he disappeared. That was in October of 1982."

"Where'd he go?" I asked.

The old man shrugged again. "Your guess is as good as mine. For many years, he lived on the streets. I suppose the voices in his head were more real than anything else to him. Then, about five years ago, I was at the Seattle Center when I heard someone playing the music of that guy who became rich performing for kids—Raffi is his name. 'Bananaphone' is my favorite song of his. Ever heard of it?"

Marcy and I shook our heads. Majykowski frowned, as if our response confirmed yet another problem with our upbringing.

"No matter. He was playing a tuba, of all things. It was Sir Lionel! I walked up and said hello. And you know what he said?"

"Who the hell are you?" Marcy guessed, with a smile.

"Not quite," Majykowski said. "He asked me if I would mind buying him a Big Mac. I didn't mind. I like to think it was his way of saying he remembered me. He ate three Big Macs, and we actually had a fairly lucid conversation. I've tried to keep an eye on him ever since."

"What about his parents?" Marcy asked.

"Both dead." Majykowski's eyes glittered. "He's never even asked about them. And I've never told him."

"I wonder if he knows," I said.

"He might," Majykowski said.

"What's his real name?" I asked.

The professor shook his head. "Sir Lionel *is* his real name now. Mention his old name, and it only enrages him. He's asked me to keep it a secret; he may be disturbed, but I made him a promise. It's a shame, really. He was such a wonderful cellist—the most talented young person I'd ever heard. That is, until I heard you."

I took another bite of sandwich and frowned at his praise. *A lot of good it's done me so far.* But as bad as my life seemed, it was nowhere near as bad as Sir Lionel's. And I didn't hear anything but the usual single voice in my head; I figured when I started hearing two, I'd start worrying.

"So here is my proposal to you, my young cello player," Majykowski said, his gray eyes bright as he pushed away from the counter. "I will become your teacher; you will become my student—perhaps my last. Hah! That is a thought! And if we're lucky and you don't go crazy on me like a few of my other students, then maybe if you're good enough, we will enter you in the Volt competition in the spring and see what is what."

"Sounds like a plan," I said. "What's in it for me?"

Majykowski smiled, his face coming alive with wrinkles. "The winner gets $10,000, a music scholarship, and a new Apple computer. Runner-up gets $5,000."

"I'm always interested in money," I said. It suddenly

crossed my mind that just because Mom was gone, it didn't mean I had to stay put in Seattle. Ten thousand dollars could buy even a fourteen-year-old a certain amount of freedom—maybe enough to go back to California and rent a place near the beach. *I could buy the best surfboard—*

"It won't work," I said with a shake of my head, remembering the obvious. "I don't have the money for lessons. And my mom, well, she isn't really in a position to pay, either."

Marcy started to say something, but Majykowski shushed her. He ran his wrecked fingers through his hair as he stared at me; it made me uncomfortable. He seemed to be looking inside me, seeing things I'd just as soon keep hidden. I stared back, to make him stop. Whatever it was he saw, he finally shrugged.

"I don't work for free—against my religion. But I'm willing to trade."

"Trade?" I was suddenly suspicious. "Are you some kind of a pervert?" I decided to ask it straight out, just to be clear.

Majykowski let out a sigh and shook his head grimly. "I suppose it's a sign of the times. I have been accused of many sins," he said with a shake of his white mane, "but that is not one of them. I talk with your mother if you want; she can talk with mothers and fathers of my former students—it's no problem. What I was thinking was, as a trade, you work on my boat and wash the motorcycle."

"You have a bike?"

"Yes. BMW. Very fast. Anyway, you would help out with things like that."

"Like, help out how much?"

"Two-hour lesson, one hour of work."

Marcy watched my face as I thought about it. I wondered if I should tell Majykowski that my life was a mess and that I was not the talented cellist he seemed to think I was but just a loser, plain and simple. I couldn't even guarantee what was going to happen in the next hour, let alone the next week, so how could I commit to lessons? I was about to say no when Marcy interrupted.

"Yes, Mr. Majykowski, Jace agrees to everything—with one condition," she said.

Majykowski raised his eyebrows.

"You have to teach me as well."

Majykowski looked at me for an okay.

"Yeah." I surrendered. "We're, um, partners. You want me, you get her, too."

Majykowski looked up as if seeking an answer from above. "I suppose you are poor, too?" he said glumly.

"Oh no, my dad's loaded," Marcy replied. "He'll pay whatever you want. Charge double, if you want; that way, it'll cover Jace's lessons, too."

Majykowski threw back his head and laughed. "All right, I give up. It is done and done."

He held out his hand for each of us to shake. But Marcy shook her head and made a fist. Majykowski gave her a quizzical look, then copied her. She smiled and bumped his fist with hers. Then it was my turn.

"You brought your cellos," Majykowski boomed, jumping to his feet. "Why don't we begin now? You just play for me, taking turns, while I listen and learn. Marty first."

"Marcy," I said.

"Ah, yes, Marly," he said.

I started to correct him, but I stopped when I saw the evil smile playing on his lips. *He isn't going to make it easy for her.* There was pay and payback, and Majykowski was going to make sure he got a little bit of payback from Marcy.

I think it turned out to be the best afternoon of my life, and yet I could have so easily blown it—I could have left Marcy on the ferry or refused to get off the boat or told Majykowski to get stuffed. But I didn't. Don't get me wrong; it didn't make up for what had happened the day before. It couldn't ever erase the mess with my mom—nothing would change that. But it helped ease the pain a bit.

I'd also learned something: if I'd tried to go it alone, none of those good things would have happened, and I owed it all to Marcy. I was sure going to miss her if something crazy happened and I won that contest, then went off to some big-time music school.

18

We caught the 9:10 p.m. ferry back to Seattle, but unlike on the morning trip, the ferry was now crowded with weekenders heading back to the city. I didn't really feel like playing my cello any more that day, especially on the ferry for money. But I was never one to pass up an opportunity.

Marcy scanned the cabin. "Hey. Let's go upstairs and just play for us," she suggested. "What do you think?" She saw me hesitate. "We can play next week when we come over for our lesson," Marcy said, "and you can keep my half. Whaddya say?"

That settled it. "Deal," I said, with a tired smile. We found a place out of the wind, underneath the cover of the deck. There was just a handful of other passengers huddled together against the chill night breeze blowing off the water as the ferry headed towards the docks of Seattle.

"What do you want to play?" I asked, pulling Ruby out. I tuned up each peg until it was perfect.

"How about we start with 'Satin Doll'?" Marcy replied.

"Never heard of it."

"It's an old jazz tune," she said. "My grandmother loved it and played the recording all the time. I'll run through it once, and then you can join in."

You could tell from the first note that Marcy really loved this song. The warm, clear sounds from her cello floated across the deck, and I could see people turning in our direction, pointing and smiling. Yeah, it was that good. She looked up when she was near the end, but instead of playing along with her, I decided to do my best baby string bass impression. I plucked the strings, picking out a lower line underneath, reinforcing the beat with my notes.

"Wow, that was great," Marcy said when we finished. "I really loved how you played that bass line. Now it's your turn to pick."

"How about some old time, um, Jay-Z?" I said with a laugh. "You know, for a little change of pace."

"Jay-Z on a cello?" Marcy asked, wrinkling her nose. "That just seems wrong, somehow."

"Listen and learn," I said. Now, I suppose most people think there's all sorts of music. But to me, there are really only two kinds: good and bad. That's all that matters, not the style and not the performer. I considered for a few seconds, then pulled my bow across the strings and began one of Jay-Z's tunes.

With hip hop and rap, it's not about melody; you'd be hard pressed to whistle along with any of the songs. But the rhythms and the pulse, the pops and the way everything interacts with the words are what makes it all work. Even though a cello's meant to play notes, it also does a pretty good job on rhythm, 'specially if you treat your bow more like a drumstick. I started by slapping the cello for emphasis, picking out the rhythms and cadence of "Ride or Die." When I was done, I leaned back in my seat and pulled off my sweatshirt. I was hot, despite the cool night air.

Marcy clapped with delight. She started to say something but then stopped, her eyes growing wider.

"And what's going on here?"

The three muscle-bound turds from my first day at school were standing in the shadows out beyond the cover of the sundeck. They were wearing long-sleeved T-shirts and baseball caps, brim backwards, and none of them were smiling.

"So the fag and his little friend can play music," said the guy I'd nailed with the quarters. "How cute. Where's your other geek friend with the red hair?"

"It was Jay-Z, loser," Marcy said quietly, her face pale. "Elvis *and* his parents will be right back."

I glanced around; the deck was deserted. Whatever the reason—too cold or too late or whatever—while I had been playing, everyone had crowded down below.

"Look, you guys," I stuttered, forcing a smile, "about that problem at school—it was a stupid thing to do. I mean, I stuck my nose in where it wasn't wanted. So let's just say we chill. And that punch, well, I'm such a pussy, I'm sure it didn't really hurt. But if it did, feel free to kick the crap out of me now; just leave Marcy alone."

The guy Marcy had called a loser seemed to think about what I'd just said. Or maybe it just showed how slowly his brain worked. He glanced over his shoulder at his two clone buddies.

"First of all," he said, "we were never properly intro-
duced. Loser? That just won't do, will it, between friends
and all? My name is Adrian. And these are my two friends,
Bobby and Turk."

I fought back a chuckle. The whole situation was un-
real. I mean, what were the odds of running into these three
guys on the ferry instead of at school? One in a thousand?
And then, what were the odds that absolutely no one else
would be around? I guess I'm just lucky or something.

"Well, awesome to meet you guys," I said. "Right,
Marcy?"

"Gag me," Marcy said.

"What did she say?" Adrian looked around the deck.
"French-kiss me? Is that what you said?"

"Yeah, I heard it," Bobby said, nodding his head.

Marcy moved closer to me for protection. But I wasn't
sure what I was going to be able to do this time. I didn't
have a roll of quarters handy.

"Now, guys, this isn't cool. I mean, really. Can't we
just let it go?" I raised my bow like it was a fencing sword,
ready to jab if they made a move in our direction; it was
pathetic.

Adrian smiled. Then he grabbed the end of my bow,
wrenched it away, and broke it in half. He poked me in the
chest, his eyes bulging with sudden rage, and screamed,
"I'll tell you what isn't cool: being attacked by a punk like
you! If you hadn't pulled that shitty stunt with the quarters,
I wudda knocked your frickin' head off!"

He didn't give me a chance to reply, but followed up
with a quick stomach punch. Then he grabbed Ruby as I

doubled over. "Payback's a bitch, bitch, ain't it?" he sneered.

"Put it back!" Marcy screamed.

"First *you* gotta give us something," Adrian purred, "and maybe then I'll hand it over."

"Okay," Marcy said, her voice flat. "Whatever."

I looked up with alarm when I heard that. I was still having trouble catching my breath, but in the distance, I could see a hill covered with houses. That meant we were in Elliott Bay; just a little longer, and they'd have to let us go.

"No," I wheezed. "I can't let you do it."

"It's all right, Stringz," Marcy said softly. "I can handle it."

I slipped off my glasses and tossed them into my open cello case. It was hard to stand up straight, but I did it. "So you made your point, man. We're even now. Leave Marcy alone, give me my cello back, and we'll just forget about it."

Adrian glanced over his shoulder, probably noticing how close we were getting to the docks. He began to rotate his shoulders, gripping Ruby's neck so tight, his knuckles turned white. "What'd you say, pussy?" Adrian snarled at me.

"You heard him, damn you!" Marcy yelled. "Give him back his cello!"

"I got a better idea!" Adrian shrieked, his lips flecked with spit. "And here it is: if you want this piece of shit so badly, go get it!" Then he whirled around and flung my cello over the side rail into the darkness.

I think my heart stopped as I watched my cello—the

most important thing in my life—disappear. And then everything seemed to happen all at once.

Marcy screamed, "You son of a bitch!" and flung herself at Adrian.

"Oh, man," I heard Turk say, "that was wicked."

Bobby chimed in with one word: "Cool."

And before I had a chance to think about it, I bolted across the deck and did a Superman leap over the railing.

19

First of all, I wasn't afraid—not really. I mean, it's not like I haven't been around water before. And I've surfed some fairly big waves. But I'd never jumped out of the equivalent of the third-story window of something the size of a parking garage going fifteen or twenty miles per hour on water. I guess what I'm trying to say is I'd never done anything this crazy before.

As I fell past the lighted passenger deck windows, I realized that diving headfirst into the water probably wasn't a good idea. I could feel myself turning over anyway, so I just tucked in my chin and knees and did a kind of midair somersault. When I spotted the line of lights on the shoreline, I straightened my legs and pointed my toes toward the water. And then I hit the water. It felt like concrete, and the shock went all the way up to the top of my head. My legs collapsed and my knees smacked into my chest, knocking the air out of my lungs.

Next, I felt another shock: *COLD!* My brain shrieked. I'd never been in water like this—so bitterly cold. It felt like a lake filled with ice; my face and bare arms were stabbed by a million tiny needles of cold. I fought back an impulse to gasp—good thing, too, because I was still plummeting deeper into the water. One breath would've filled my lungs with water, and that would've been the end of me.

But despite the shock and pain and cold, I also felt something else, like I was stuck in some sort of gigantic Jacuzzi. The water all around me was swirling and vibrating, and that's when the image of a huge propeller flashed across my mind. I may have temporarily survived the leap over the side, but there was still a good chance of being sucked into the ferry's propeller. So I did what any sane person would do—I panicked. I began to claw and kick; I might have even done some underwater screaming—if that's possible.

Then, just when I thought my lungs were going to explode, I broke the surface. I took a deep breath and then barfed, took another gasp of air and barfed again. Yeah, I was alive. But I wasn't out of danger. The ferry was right there in front of me: a huge, moving, massive wall so close I could touch it. I had to get away from it—*now*.

I kicked and began swimming hard, trying for a sorry-ass Michael Phelps impression. I probably made it a dozen strokes before I got caught again in turbulence from the propellers, which picked me up and flipped me around. And then, just like that, I was alone, staring at the ferry as it receded into the distance. That's when I started waving my arms, yelling and screaming; I'm sure I looked crazy, and maybe by then I was. But at least I hadn't been chopped into human salsa.

And then it hit me like a slap: *Where was Ruby?* I turned around, treading water and scanning for her, then caught the reflection of something shiny. As I swam towards it, I knew I didn't have more than a few minutes to find her. The water was so cold, my arms and legs were already going numb, and if I didn't start heading to the shore soon, I'd never make it. But as I bobbed over a wave in the darkness, there she was, floating high in the water, waiting for me, her wet surfaces reflecting the moonlight. It was just plain dumb luck. I took a couple of quick strokes, then reached out and pulled her close. "Shit," I murmured.

Okay, I know I'm a dork for pulling that stunt. I mean, I knew Ruby was just a cheap cello—just a mutt of a brand, with nothing like the pedigree of Elvis's fancy violin. But this was *my* cello, the most valuable thing I owned. And dumb as it sounds, Ruby was more family to me than anyone else. After all we'd been through together, she was the only thing I could count on.

As I floated there, clutching my precious cello, I felt more peaceful than I had in a long time. It was like all my hurt and disappointment were washing away with the tides. I felt so quiet and safe there in the dark water, I didn't want it to end.

Dying never even crossed my mind.

20

I read once that right before you die, you travel through a tunnel. At the end of it, there's a bright light. Beyond it waits a crowd of your loved ones who've already passed over. I guess that's supposed to be heaven. I sure didn't expect a crowd to be waiting for me when I died—just my grandma. But if I was almost dead, I'd skipped the tunnel part entirely, even though I could see a bright light. I'd also figured that by the time you're on your way to heaven, it'd be painless, but I still felt really cold and my cheek hurt a lot. Then it occurred to me that maybe I was heading the opposite direction. I really didn't care, either, because I was so cold, the fires of hell would've felt good—at least for a little while.

But I heard someone yelling before I had a chance to really ponder my final destination. So I blinked, and for some reason, that seemed to help; the shadows and lights started making sense, and I realized I was still alive. I blinked again, and Marcy came into focus. She was hovering over me, looking like a wet dog, her hair hanging down over her eyes. I could tell she'd been crying, because her eyes were red, and she said something I couldn't make out. I tried to say something, but my voice didn't seem to be working and my throat felt like it had been sandpapered. Then she said something again, and this time I got it.

"Damn you, Jace Adams," she said, her teeth chattering.

I was strapped to some sort of bed on wheels, and someone I couldn't see was pushing me down a hallway. Marcy was trotting along beside me with a blanket around her shoulders.

"What happened?" I rasped.

"We found you, you moron," she replied. "And just barely in time."

"You're hypothermic, son," I heard a man's voice say. "We're going to get you warmed up."

"Where's Ruby?" I gasped.

Marcy's face softened. "She saved your life. You were unconscious when they pulled you out of the water, and you had your arms locked around her like some sort of musical life raft. She was the only thing keeping you afloat."

"You're a lucky kid," added the voice.

"Despite being such a complete and utter moron," Marcy added.

I reached out and grabbed Marcy's hand. I wanted to thank her, but I couldn't get the words out. And I was so cold, my body kept jerking and shaking like somebody else controlled it. But I noticed that Marcy didn't pull her hand away; I guess that meant she wasn't as mad as she looked. Then I passed out again.

Once you've been in a hospital, even with your eyes

closed and your ears covered, you can always tell when you're in one; they have a certain signature smell—a combination of food, poop, barf, and pee mixed with antiseptic. It only takes one whiff, and you never forget it. I'd spent an afternoon in an emergency room once when we lived in Santa Rosa, when I fell off my bike and broke my wrist. So it was that blend of smells that reminded me where I was. And then I remembered my ride on the gurney with Marcy by my side and what had happened on the ferry and in the water.

I opened my eyes and looked around at the room; the glow around the closed curtain edges told me it was probably daytime. It was a typical hospital room with the usual furnishings. But then I saw something that made me feel even worse: there in a chair, resting on a towel, was Ruby, her neck broken and hanging, still attached by the strings. I felt my eyes begin to burn, and I nearly cried for the second time in a week. I was also incredibly pissed off. I couldn't wait to make Adrian and his friends pay for what they'd done.

"Well, man, I'm happy to see you, too!"

That's when I noticed a tall, young black man, nicely dressed in a suit and standing in the doorway. He could have been a banker or even a successful gangster. He was wearing sunglasses, and his hair was cropped close to his head. And then it hit me.

"Derrick?"

"That the best you can do, when you see your long-lost bro for the first time in years?"

I tried to push myself up out of bed, but my arms didn't cooperate. "Wha—what are *you* doing here?"

STRINGZ

Derrick crossed quickly over to my bed and grabbed me in a bear hug. I squeezed back as hard as I could with my weak, shaky arms. "That's better, little bro," he said. "That's much better."

The last time I'd seen Derrick was a couple of years ago when I was buying a hot dog at Venice Beach. Something jabbed me in the back and a voice whispered, "Stick 'em up, mo-fo." I knew it was him, though. I mean, who in their right mind would try and rob some punk kid in the middle of the day except my crazy bro, Derrick? By then, he'd been out of jail for six months or so and out on his own, making money any way he could, I guess. At the time, he was wearing baggy pants and a tight sleeveless shirt; his head was shaved, and it made him look older than he was, worn down.

But looking at him now, I could see Derrick had moved up in the world since then. Instead of dressing like a gangsta, he looked like Wall Street—mighty fine. He'd even let his hair grow back a bit. I took in the bling around his neck, the diamond stud in his ear, and the fancy knock-off Rolex on his wrist, and figured whatever he'd gotten into must pay pretty well.

"Woo—hee," Derrick said, pinching his nose and stepping back from the hug. "You're gonna stink up my new suit—three grand at Saks," he said, flicking his thumbs under the lapels. One thing about Derrick, he'd always liked nice-looking clothes. Not to mention nice-looking girls . . . and cars. . . .

"Sorry, man," I said, "I took a little swim."

147

Derrick's gaze hardened. "So I heard. I didn't 'spect to be seeing you this way, but you made the late news and I figured now was as good a time as any to let you know I'm around."

"Mom left." I blurted it like a punk kid.

Derrick eyed me for a moment. "Is that why you decided to kill yourself?"

"I wasn't trying to kill myself!"

"No? Coulda fooled me and everyone else—except that cute little girlfriend of yours. What's her name?"

"Marcy. And she's not my girlfriend."

"Yeah, right."

"Yeah, and it had nothin' to do with Mom," I insisted, pushing myself up from the bed. I didn't realize I was still so weak; my arms began to shake from the effort, and I fell back on the pillows and closed my eyes. I had nothing to hide from Derrick, so I told him the truth about what happened on the ferry. Then I pointed at my cello.

"So you went in after it?" he asked.

"What else could I do?" I sighed. "I wasn't looking to star in a new Jackass movie or somethin'. I had to try and—"

He held up both hands. "I get it," he said. "No need to explain it."

And I knew he really *did* understand. He was my brother, and he was the one who'd taught me to respect musical instruments.

"Who were they?" His voice had a menacing edge.

I shook my head. I wasn't ready to give them up—not yet. I'd already started cooking up some payback for those jerks. Maybe start with their cars; I'd learned a thing or two about torching stuff. Or maybe I'd go the subtle route and start by signing them up for porn magazines that their parents would find—simple things like that. There were a hundred ways I could make their lives miserable, and they'd never even know it was me. Or maybe I'd just do nothing for now.

Word would get out about what they'd done. Giving me crap was one thing, but throwing my cello off the ferry was way over the top. Besides, Marcy no doubt was already spreading the word. One thing I'd learned about her—she was fearless. It was actually kind of scary sometimes.

"In case you're wondering about Mom," I said, "she took off with—"

"I know all about it, bro. Bernice told me," Derrick interrupted. He shook his head. "I'm surprised it didn't happen sooner. Mom was always a bi—" He paused when he saw the look on my face.

"I meant to say, she was always the restless type, if you know what I mean. I guess I got my restless nature from her."

"Her boyfriend said I was *baggage*," I complained. "Made it sound like I'm nothing more than garbage."

Suddenly, Derrick seemed to grow in size. He glowered, his fists clenched. "That son of a bitch," Derrick growled. "I have half a mind to take a little drive to Denver and teach that prick some manners. Look, don't ever say or even think that about yourself. You're not only disrespecting yourself, you're disrespecting me, because you and me are family. And nobody gets to do that—not even you."

That was the Derrick I knew and loved, and man, it was great to have him back. I didn't even realize how much I'd missed him. I even thought about saying so, but I was so tired suddenly—more than I'd ever been before. Strange how a little swim in ice-cold water can take so much out of you.

"All right, big bro," I said. "So what brings you all the way to Seattle?"

"I live here," he said.

"You what?" I couldn't hide my surprise.

"Been here a year already," he replied.

"Does Mom know?" I asked, wondering if maybe that was part of the reason she'd picked Seattle this time.

Derrick shook his head no. "We haven't talked since, you know . . . " His voice trailed off. "Anyway, I'm not doing what I was doing before. I'm in the music business now. I'm an agent for a record producer in L.A. Also got me my own little label. I'm looking for talent in the Northwest. But what'd I find instead? My own li'l bro."

I fought back a yawn. "You legit now?"

Derrick smiled and nodded, the diamond in his front tooth sparkling. "Legit as a politician or a preacher," he said with a laugh.

I shook my head, trying to clear the fog from my brain. It was all too much to take in. I'd lost a mom and found a lost brother, all in the space of about two days. I wondered what would be next—getting kidnapped by aliens? Find dear old dad knocking on the door? After this, nothing would surprise me.

"Why don't you sleep some, bro," I heard Derrick say. "Bernie's got my number. Your girlfriend, too, in case you want to talk."

I started to tell him again that she wasn't my girlfriend, but I couldn't seem to make my mouth work. Just before I fell asleep, I thought I heard Derrick say, "I love you, li'l bro."

Probably just dreaming.

21

So it's against the law to jump off a ferryboat. *Well, duh.* I guess it would've been different if I'd jumped in after a baby or something like that—in other words, a human. But trying to save a cheap cello? No way. When I tried explaining it to the cop who showed up at the hospital to question me, he shook his head, saying, "You gotta be kidding me."

It was a week after I'd made the evening news. Derrick and the law still weren't exactly buddy-buddy, so he decided to skip my court hearing. Bernice was working, so it was just me, Marcy, and Elvis, sitting there in court with Professor Majykowski, his wife, and Sir Lionel behind us in the audience. Elvis's dad was my attorney. I'd lucked out; he was doing it for free. And it sounded like he was the man, according to what I'd heard.

"He's managed to get guys off who were accused of murder," Elvis had said proudly.

"I'll keep that in mind after I'm done killing Adrian and his two trolls," I said. Elvis managed to laugh and look worried at the same time. I guess he wasn't sure I was kidding. I wasn't sure, either.

❦

So there I was in court, sitting there in one of Derrick's too-big-on-me suits, trying to act like I was sorry for causing trouble. Mr. Goldberg assured the judge that I was an upstanding young man and that I'd just reacted in the heat of the moment to an outrageous and cruel act. He said that if anything as disturbing as this ever happened again, I'd be sure to seek help from the proper authorities rather than take matters into my own foolish hands.

"Is that right, young man?" the judge asked. Her gray hair was stacked up nearly as high as Elvis's Afro, and she wore bright red lipstick; her face showed a lot of wear, and yet her eyes were warm and kind. I hoped that meant something. Then I noticed Marcy motioning for me to stand up.

"Well, uh, ma'am," I said, jumping to my feet and smoothing down the front of my jacket. "I do appreciate all that Mr. Goldberg is doing for me. But this is a court of law, right?"

She nodded. If anything, her eyes seemed to grow even brighter.

"And I should tell the truth, right?"

"Unless you want to end up in even more trouble than you already are, young man, you had best be truthful," she replied.

"That's what I thought," I said quickly. "Well, to be honest with you, I'm not sure what I'd do if the same thing happened again. See, it wasn't just any old musical instrument he tossed over that railing; that was, well, Ruby. I've had her a long time, and she's been the only person left who I could trust."

"Person?"

"Yes, Judge, *person*," came the response from behind me.

"And who might you be?" the judge asked, shifting her focus behind me to the small band of spectators.

"Aldo Majykowski, at your service. I'm this young man's music teacher." He waved at Marcy. "And Marcy's, too."

"That's all well and good, Mr. Majykowski," the judge said, "but I don't like people interrupting the proceedings in my courtroom. If you persist, I'll have you removed."

"Yes, your honor," Majykowski said, "but let me just tell you that there is a wonderful bond between a fine musician and his or her instrument. Jace's Ruby wasn't worth much money, but together they made a sound that was from heaven. For this boy, that cello *was* a person. Please believe me."

"I believe I will clear the courtroom and fine you for contempt if you utter one more syllable." The judge tapped her pen in time with each word.

Majykowski opened his mouth, closed it, swallowed, gave her a courtly European bow, and then sat down. His wife leaned over and kissed him on the cheek.

"Well, Mr. Adams. How do you plead to the charges?"

"Guilty, ma'am, I mean, Judge."

"All right. I'll waive any jail time, and you'll be on probation for six months. I'm sentencing you to forty hours of community service. If you don't get into any more trouble, all record of this will be expunged when you're eighteen."

I started to reply, but Mr. Goldberg placed a hand on my shoulder and squeezed. I got the message and kept quiet. "Thank you, Judge Miller. We appreciate your forbearance."

"That was an unusually lenient sentence," Mr. Goldberg said as we stepped out into the hallway. "Judge Miller has a well-deserved reputation for being extremely tough."

"Forty hours' community service doesn't sound so lenient to me," I complained.

"Beats cooling your heels for a month or two in juvie," Elvis said.

"I'm still not happy about this," Marcy whispered, jabbing me in the side. I'd still refused to tell anyone who'd tossed Ruby in the drink. But that hadn't stopped Marcy from telling just about anyone who would listen. The cops had taken down names, but since there weren't any other witnesses and I wasn't talking, they didn't do anything. I guess wrecking cellos wasn't that big of a deal to them.

"Why didn't you say something in there?" Marcy asked. "This isn't your fault."

"Derrick has a plan that'll teach them a lesson," I assured her.

"Is this another one of those stupid macho man plans?" she asked. "If it involves blood, I'm going to tell Mr. Goldberg what's going on."

"Nope, no blood," I lied.

Derrick hadn't told me what he had in mind, but I

hoped it not only involved a lot of blood but also some piss-your-pants terror to go with it. He'd listened to some of my plans for revenge and pronounced them all stupid when he'd joined me and Bernice for dinner a few days after I got out of the hospital. I'd invited Elvis, too; it was almost like a little family.

"There's getting mad," Derrick explained, "and there's getting even without getting caught. What would you rather do?"

"Get even," Elvis and I said in unison.

Derrick fist-bumped me while Bernice shoved Elvis in agreement.

"You listen to your brother," Bernice said, wagging a fork at me. "You've already done one stupid thing. I'm not sure I could survive another. Not to mention how upset I'd be if you got the King here in trouble, too," she said, motioning towards Elvis.

"Oh," I said. "I didn't think you cared that much about me."

"Oh, she doesn't," Derrick said, his own fork waving. "She's just trying to be polite."

Bernice smiled and slapped Derrick's open palm. "I don't know what your momma had against this boy," she said. "I kinda like him—reminds me of my fourth husband."

"Fourth?" I said. "I thought you only had three husbands."

"Musta lost count," Bernice cackled.

"Whatever happens," Elvis chimed in, "I want to be in on it. I mean, it all started with me. I think it should end there, too."

Derrick gave Elvis a once-over, but I could tell he was considering it. "I'll keep it in mind, Red."

Ɑ

"So now what?" Marcy asked as we stood outside the courthouse.

When I didn't respond immediately, she elbowed me in the side.

"Hello? Anyone home?"

"Ouch," I said. "You didn't have to do that. I was just, um, thinking."

Before Marcy had a chance to be nosy, Professor Majykowski wrapped us in a bear hug and said, "How about some adult beverages and pizza? We drink the adult beverages; you children eat the pizza. I buy."

"I know just the place," Sir Lionel said, pushing into the mix. He didn't smell very good, but everyone was too polite to say anything. "It is the best pizza west of Chicago on Planet Earth in the Milky Way Galaxy. It is also run by my mother's cousin's son-in-law's brother."

"Your what?" we all said in unison.

"I just call him Sidney," Sir Lionel said with a smile. "He lets me eat for free."

I slapped Sir Lionel on the back. He pulled away and made a face. "Free," I said with a laugh. "That's my favorite kind, too!"

Later that night, I couldn't sleep, and it wasn't just the fourteen slices of pizza that I'd eaten. In a lot of ways, I felt like I was back out in the bay, treading water. Except this time, Ruby couldn't save me.

I rolled off the bed and turned on the light. Normally, when I had trouble sleeping, I'd play my cello. But Ruby was ruined, and I was too exhausted to feel anything but the ache of that loss. Now, I had nearly $500 stashed in the leg of my bed, but unless I was incredibly lucky, that wasn't going to be nearly enough for a decent cello, a new bow, and a case—not even close. I knew I could ask Derrick for a loan, but I didn't feel right about doing that. All this meant that I was stuck; I was on my own this time, and I needed some kind of plan.

I grabbed a blanket and dragged a kitchen chair outside so I could watch the sky. And except for a siren wailing in the distance, it was just about as quiet as it ever gets in Seattle. As I sat there, I tried to make some sense out of everything.

Mom always got restless every four or five months, and then we'd move to someplace new. If things got tough, it was *time to move*. Bad job, *move again*. Bad apartment, *move on*. Creepy landlord, *move the hell away*. And on it went, which made change and me into traveling buddies. But the thing is, deep down, change terrified me. And I'd never realized how afraid of it I'd been. I suppose I'd learned to keep it hidden, learned to use it as fuel for my music, but the fear was still there. I'd always been afraid we didn't have enough money or afraid my mom would die and leave me alone. I was afraid my brother didn't love me, afraid the kids down the street were going to hurt me. I was afraid—well, of just about everything. I'd become so used to it—being afraid—that I forgot it was even there.

But now, for the first time in forever, that fear had actually left me—because I had Bernice and Derrick watching out for me and because Elvis and Marcy were my friends. And best of all, for the first time ever, I had a place to stay for as long as I wanted. I pulled the blanket tight around my shoulders, relaxed, and fell asleep.

22

I went back to school on Tuesday, and except for a head cold and a sore ankle from hitting the water wrong, I was basically okay. I didn't run into Adrian or his buddies—probably a good thing. I wasn't looking for trouble, but I was so pissed off at them, I'm not sure what I'd have done if I'd seen them in the hallway. And they were obviously avoiding me, considering what'd happened.

Bernice was back to her lovable old crabby self, but now I could see through all the sarcasm and bluster—most of the time, anyway. I still didn't want to cross her, though. I wasn't that foolish.

And as it turned out, Mr. Whitehead wasn't a complete dickhead, either. I was dreading what he'd do when I showed up in orchestra class without my cello. But instead of dishing a load of crap, he was waiting for me with a loaner cello.

"It's just until you get a new instrument," he said. "I read about the ferry incident. Anyway, we had this old one back in the storage room and it'll have to do for now. We don't have money to refurbish it, but I did replace the strings for you."

"Thanks a lot," I choked, surprised that he even knew the story.

"And Adams?"

"Yessir."

"I, uh, want you playing on the first stand with Marcy. She's still first chair, but you're second. I presume that won't be a problem. . . . " He trailed off, almost as if he expected some kind of negative response from me.

"Nossir," was all I said.

Then he dismissed me with a nod.

I wasn't used to changing my opinion about people once it was set, but I realized that I might have to make an exception in Dickhead's case. And he was right about the condition of the cello. It was so messed up, it made me take back all the bad things I'd ever thought about Ruby. Compared to this piece of crap, she'd sounded like a Stradivarius. But still, it was a cello. It wasn't broken, and the price was right. It'd have to do for now.

Meanwhile, my ankle felt strong enough to start running again by the end of the week. I didn't expect any slack from Coach Ford, and he didn't disappoint me. After my first practice back, he called me into his office.

"What did you do, now?" Elvis asked when he heard.

"Nothing, honest."

"Why don't I believe you?" he laughed.

After cooling down and stretching with the team, I pulled on my sweats, grabbed my bag and the case for the instrument I'd nicknamed Frankenstein, and then trudged into Coach Ford's office.

"Sit down, Mr. Adams," he barked.

I flopped into the chair, hoping he was going to ask about my ankle. But no such luck.

"Do you remember how we first met?" he asked.

"How could I forget?"

"Have you had any trouble from those guys since that time?" Coach didn't smile, but the way he stared at me made me think he already knew everything that had happened on that ferry and exactly who was involved. I knew it was just a trick, or I should say, I hoped it was just a trick. And just because he was acting like he cared about me and what happened to me, I certainly wasn't going to suddenly spill my guts to him. He was my coach, not my friend. And he wasn't my dad.

"Nossir. Haven't seen them since then. Everything's been cool."

Coach Ford continued to stare at me. I knew if I spoke first, I'd lose it. So I bit the inside of my cheek and stayed quiet. He finally broke eye contact and sighed. *Gotcha*, I thought to myself.

"You know, son," Mr. Ford said, "someday you're going to have to trust *somebody*."

He was right about that. I may have been fourteen, but I wasn't stupid. "Yessir," I said, agreeing with him. It just wasn't going to be him.

"If you ever need help, I hope you'll come to me," he said.

"You got it," I lied.

He nodded, then slumped back in his chair, looking tired. He knew I was lying, and it disappointed him. "Glad to have you back, Adams," he said. "You're all right."

"Uh, thanks, Coach."

"You aren't planning any more excitement, are you?"

"Nossir."

"Better not," he growled. "Now get on home."

" 'Night, Coach," I said as I stood up.

He waved me away, pulled his chair up close to his desk, and opened a notebook.

I glanced back as I left the room; he was just sitting there, motionless, pen in hand, staring down at the blank sheet of paper inside.

23

"Got that foreign lunatic music teacher of yours on the damn phone," Bernice roared early Saturday morning, kicking at my door.

"All right," I yelled back. I lay for a moment under my blanket and smiled. There were some things you could always count on. A cranky Bernice before her first cup of coffee and cigarette was one of them. It took me just a minute to put on some sweats and grab the phone.

"I meet you in town today," Mr. Majykowski said, without any hello. "No lessons. Ten sharp. First and Cherry. Bring your girlfriend along."

"She's not my girlfriend," I said, but Mr. Majykowski had already hung up.

"What is it now?" Bernice growled. She was sitting at the kitchen table in a bright pink fluffy bathrobe, sipping coffee and reading the newspaper.

"No lesson today," I said, with a puzzled shrug. "Mr. Majykowski wants to meet me downtown."

"I like that old fool," Bernice said. "I just don't like it when he calls so early in the morning."

Yeah, me, too. I wondered what he had in mind. Before I went back to my room, I called Marcy and told her about Majykowski's change of plans.

"Any idea what's going on?" she asked.

"Nope," I replied. "He didn't say."

"There's a McDonald's across the street. I'll meet you there about 9:45. And you're buying breakfast." She hung up before I had a chance to protest.

"I didn't realize your cute little girlfriend was invited, too," Bernice said, her face hidden by the newspaper.

I just sighed and stomped back to my bedroom to get dressed.

At ten o'clock, Majykowski stood impatiently on the corner, glancing at his watch as Marcy and I walked up. "You're two minutes late," he complained, glaring at me as the wind whipped his white hair and beard and I finished my last bite of sausage sandwich.

Majykowski turned and walked halfway down the block, not even bothering to see if we were following. He went through the revolving glass door of one of the tall glass office buildings and walked right past the security desk without even slowing down. The guard didn't seem to mind, until he saw Marcy and me; then he started to get up out of his chair. But before he could stop us, Majykowski barked, "They're with me," and the guard settled back in his chair.

"How'd you do that?" Marcy asked when we caught up to the teacher at the elevator doors.

"They know me here." Majykowski dismissed it with a conductor's wave of the hand. We got in the elevator, and

Majykowski pressed an unlabeled button at the top of the control panel, then entered a series of numbers, using a small LCD screen beneath the panel.

"Where're we going?" I asked.

Majykowski just smiled. A moment later, the elevator doors opened. I yawned to clear my ears and glanced over at Marcy. She was staring, wide-eyed.

"Maestro," came the greeting. "And you brought your friends. How delightful."

We stepped out of the elevator into an expansive room. "What the hell?" I exclaimed.

"It's called a penthouse, dummy," Marcy whispered.

Across the room, a thin, gray-haired man waved from behind a boat-sized desk. "Under normal circumstances, I'd get up to greet you, but as you can see . . . " he rolled out from behind the desk in a wheelchair.

Majykowski rushed forward and grasped the man's hand. "So kind of you to see us, my dear Edward. Let me introduce two of my students: Jace and Marcy."

"My pleasure," said the man. He pushed a control at the end of his armrest, wheeled over closer to us, and then offered his hand for us to shake. "I'm Edward Blue. It's good to meet you both."

I mumbled something in response, more puzzled than before. Marcy shook his hand first, then I did. I had no idea why we were there. *Okay, nice old white guy in a wheelchair. Sorry about the old and wheelchair, but what's going on? What is he to us?*

"Let's get down to business," Mr. Blue announced, driving his wheelchair to a sitting area near the windows.

As I settled into the couch, I looked around. Penthouse office: check. Secure elevator stop: check. Expensive-looking paintings on the walls: check. Floor-to-ceiling windows looking out over Elliott Bay and the Olympic Mountains: check. This guy was definitely rich, maybe even mega-rich, if this stuff was real and he owned the building.

"Aldo and I go way back," Mr. Blue began, speaking directly to me. That's when I heard his soft accent, which reminded me of Mr. Majykowski's. "He told me about your, ah, adventure on the ferry. He also mentioned that you are a talented musician in need of an instrument suited to your considerable talents."

I looked at Mr. Majykowski, who spread his arms and gave a modest nod of his head. I hadn't noticed it before, but sitting on the floor next to Mr. Majykowski was a green fiberglass cello case covered in scuff marks and what looked like the remnants of old labels. Mr. Blue nodded to Mr. Majykowski, who leaned forward and slid the case over to me.

I stared at first one and then the other of the two men, not knowing what to say.

Marcy broke the spell. "Yo, Stringz," she hissed under her breath. "Open it up and check it out—and don't forget to say thank you!"

I flipped open the latches, and there was the most beautiful cello I'd ever seen. I looked up. Mr. Majykowski was bouncing in his chair like a child, and Mr. Blue was beaming.

"Do you know anything about cellos, Jace?" Mr. Blue asked.

167

"What do you mean?" I replied. "I play the cello, so, yeah, sure, I know a little bit about them."

"Does the name Leandro Bisiach mean anything to you?" He was half smiling as he asked me the question.

I shook my head. As far as I knew, it could have been the name of the guy who made pizza down the street. Marcy, on the other hand, let out a slight squeal. I turned to find her open-mouthed and motionless.

Mr. Blue continued: "Bisiach was one of the finest violin and cello makers of the late nineteenth and early twentieth centuries. He ran one of the great workshops in Milan and is reputed to have obtained tools and varnish recipes used by the famous Stradivari. He produced this wonderful cello in 1899."

"No shit," I said, the words popping out of my mouth before I had a chance to stop them.

I thought Mr. Blue was going to choke. He turned red, and then he threw back his head and laughed. "Indeed, my young cellist," he said, between waves of laughter. "Indeed." He had to wipe his eyes before he could continue. "Yes, it is a very, very fine instrument. Aldo assures me that you are worthy of it."

I raised my hand, student-like.

"Yes, Jace?"

"Excuse me, Mr. Blue, I don't mean any disrespect, but I couldn't accept this. It has to be worth a fortune. . . ."

"It is," Mr. Majykowski interrupted.

"And if I lost it or it was stolen or something, I could never afford to pay you back, not in a million years."

What were they thinking? I fought back a sudden pulse

of anger and started up from my seat, ready to head for the elevator. But before I managed to take a step, Marcy grabbed the back of my jacket and pulled me back down in my seat.

"I like and admire prudence and caution," Mr. Blue said. "And I mean no disrespect. I am also not an idiot. This cello is heavily insured, and I know you would never do anything to harm it. But this instrument deserves to be played. And I want you to play it."

"But I just couldn't," I stuttered. "I'm not—"

"Good enough?" Mr. Blue asked, his eyes sparkling. "I trust Aldo, and let me assure you, if you're as good as he says, you are indeed good enough. And I am not referring just to your talent, which I'm told is immense, but to something even more important."

"What might that be?" I asked.

"Character, young man," he said.

"Are you an idiot?" Marcy hissed, hitting me on the shoulder. "Of course he'll take it," she said loudly.

Mr. Blue held up his hand. "There's only one condition for using this cello. I'm letting you borrow it for as long as you're one of Aldo's students. When that ends, you return the cello to me. Do you agree?"

"Yes," I said. Marcy jabbed me in the ribs, and I cleared my throat. "No problem. I mean, thank you. I'll guard it with my life. I mean, I, um, don't really know what to say."

"Say?" Mr. Blue raised an eyebrow. "You don't have to say anything. Just do. Or rather, just play. I'm an old man. I have more money than I can ever spend. Now I do what I can to nurture beauty. Play beautiful music, young man, and make the world a better place because of it. That's all I ask."

Part of me thought that what he'd just said was about the stupidest thing I'd heard in a long time. But another part of me was thrilled by his words.

"Why don't you play something, Jace," Mr. Majykowki suggested.

I looked at Mr. Blue, who nodded encouragement.

My hands trembled as I lifted the cello out of the case, extended the spike, and grabbed the bow. I took a deep breath and began to play a simple Bach piece, his *Minuet in G Major*. After the first few notes, I felt as if I'd been playing that cello all my life. In a strange way, it was as if I'd always been meant to play this awesome cello.

I don't remember much of what happened next. After I was done playing, Mr. Blue thanked me. Then we talked for a while; my mouth moved from time to time, but I had no idea what I'd said. I hope that when we left, I remembered to shake Mr. Blue's hand and thank him again for his gift. I was just stunned and kind of numb—but in a good way.

By the time I came to my senses, we were back out on the street. I was gripping the green cello case in one hand, and Mr. Majykowski had just grabbed me by the shoulders and was shaking me.

"We begin seriously next Saturday. Not much time left if you are to be ready for the Volt. I want you working on the preliminary repertoire for the audition tape."

"What are the pieces I need to play?" I asked, blinking behind my glasses.

"Two contrasting movements from the Bach *Unaccompanied Cello Suites*, Marcy said. "And Boccherini—his concerto in B flat major, the first movement. And something of your own choosing."

"That's exactly right," Mr. Majykowski agreed. "And you, Miss Marcy. I expect you to work on the same pieces for a recital that you will give in March. Just because you don't happen to be African American or Latino doesn't give you a free pass with me."

Marcy's face turned red, and she bowed her head. "Thank you, sir," she said. "I mean, thank you for not forgetting me."

"Nothing to thank me for," Majykowski growled. "You are a talented young musician. Let's see how fantastic you can become, too, ya?"

Marcy and I sat in the back of the bus on the way home. We didn't talk; each of us was occupied with our own thoughts, and the cello lay on the seat between us.

"I still can't believe it," Marcy finally said.

"What?"

"Mr. Blue. Do you know who he is?"

"No idea."

"I've heard my dad say he's just about the richest guy around. Sort of like a Warren Buffett in a wheelchair. But unlike some of these other rich guys who give money to big city orchestras or kids in Africa, Mr. Blue loves art, music and musicians."

"I thought Bill Gates was the richest guy around?"

Marcy shrugged. "Maybe so. But unlike Mr. Microsoft, Mr. Blue thinks that the way to change the world isn't through science but by getting kids to play musical instruments."

"He's kidding, right?" I snorted.

Marcy's eyes became distant. "I don't know. Think about it. Has anyone tried it this way before? What if Osama Bin Laden's dad had insisted that Osama play the flute or maybe the electric guitar? Or what if a requirement for becoming, oh, I don't know, president of the United States was that you play a violin or paint with watercolors or tap dance?"

It sounded nuts to me, but maybe Marcy had a point. I couldn't imagine what my life would be like without music, and maybe it could make a difference for other people, too.

"This is my stop," I said. I stood up and grabbed my new cello. "See you later."

Marcy didn't respond. She was just staring out the window. I hesitated for a moment and then sat back down. This time, I didn't put the cello case between us.

"What's wrong?" I asked.

"You'd better go," she said quietly.

"I'll get off at the next stop," I said.

Marcy looked away from the window and shrugged. "Well, Stringz, since you asked, I was just thinking about my dad."

"And?"

She shrugged again. "I was just wishing that he'd played a musical instrument when he was a kid. That's all."

"Why's that?"

She narrowed her eyes. "Maybe then he'd understand me—at least a little," she replied, grabbing my arm and laying her head on my shoulder.

As the bus jostled to the next stop, I listened while she told me for the first time about her problems with her dad. Whatever she did was never good enough. He always compared her to her older sister, the one who had played piano, sung in the school choir, and, oh yeah, served as student council president her senior year.

"She's also gorgeous," Marcy added.

"But you're pretty, too," I blurted.

"You aren't just saying that, are you?" Marcy was looking out the window again, but I could see her watching me in the reflection.

I shook my head. "No, I'm not just saying it to make you feel better. Seriously, I like how you look." It was lame, I know. But I couldn't think of anything else to say.

Marcy turned her heard and kissed me on the cheek. "That's the sweetest thing anyone's ever said to me," she said.

Now I really didn't know what to say, so I brought the conversation back to her dad. "So what are you going to do about this thing with your dad?"

Marcy looked back out the window. "I don't know. But I'm sick of it," she said softly.

"I hope you aren't thinking of doing anything, you know, crazy," I said.

"Like maybe becoming anorexic or bulimic or maybe cutting myself—or what about jumping off a ferry?"

173

"Yeah," I laughed nervously, "that's what I was thinking."

Marcy laughed without humor. "Don't worry. I'm going to do something that's even worse than any of those things."

Oh, crap. Here we go.

"I'm going to tell him how I feel. I'm going to tell him that I'm sick of always being compared to Amy. And I'm going to tell him that just once in my life, it would be nice if he showed a little interest in *me* and what's important to me. I may scream and yell and maybe throw a few breakable expensive objects while I'm at it."

"Wow," I breathed. "It all sounds so, I don't know—"

"Dramatic?" she finished for me.

"I was thinking more like *brave*," I said.

Marcy put her head back on my shoulder. "Thanks, Stringz," she said. "I just don't feel very brave at the moment."

We stayed together like that until we came to her stop. I'd always assumed that having a dad in your life was better than not having one, but now I wasn't so sure. It occurred to me that having a crappy dad could be just as big a problem.

"Want me to walk you home?" I asked as I followed Marcy off the bus.

She shook her head. "No, thanks. I think I need a little time alone. I'll see you later."

I watched her head off down the street. When she was out of sight, I crossed the street and caught the next bus heading in the opposite direction.

24

I'm not sure my life had ever been what you might call *normal*. But after that meeting with Mr. Blue, it quickly settled into a routine that became my new normal. Even the weather decided to get into the act, turning gray and rainy. This was the Seattle I'd heard about and expected.

I still had school every day, and afterwards, I was still running with Elvis and some other guys from the cross-country team, even though our season was over—except on Tuesdays and Thursdays. That's when I was attempting to teach violin to a bunch of seven- and eight-year-old kids at the Green Lake Community Center. That's what they came up with for my community service sentence—I mean, assignment.

I know. What the heck do I know about violin? I suppose the people handling community service assignments didn't realize that there was, in fact, any difference between the violin and the cello. But at least I wasn't teaching trumpet or harmonica or glockenspiel. And it would get my community service out of the way. That's what I figured, anyway.

Big mistake; my first class was a disaster. A dozen kids, all trying to play violins at the same time. Imagine a dozen howling cats in heat, and you'll get an idea of what it sounded like. It took most of the class time just to get all of the violins tuned and show the kids how to hold their violin and bow. And I didn't get any sympathy from Marcy and Elvis.

"Serves you right," Marcy said. "Maybe next time, you'll think twice about jumping overboard."

"Yeah," Elvis chimed in. "Bratty kids. What a nightmare."

"So you guys'll help me out?" I asked.

"Absolutely," Marcy said with a smile. "Wondered when you'd get around to it. We'll help out, right, Elvis?" Marcy jabbed him in the ribs.

"Noooo—"

Marcy jabbed him again, harder.

"I mean, yeah, sure." Elvis grimaced and rubbed his side. "Can't wait."

"Great," I replied.

Elvis was the star at my second class. He and Marcy showed up dressed like clowns—crazy hair, makeup, the whole works. But it wasn't just the costumes. Elvis brought along his violin and played a couple of simple songs, as well as snippets of Beethoven. The kids loved the music—and him. For most of them, I think it was the first time they'd ever heard a violin.

After a brief intro, we divided the kids into three groups, four kids to a teacher. By the end of that class, I had to admit I was having fun. There were even a couple of kids in my group who reminded me of, well, me. I wondered if Derrick would be willing to help me scare up a couple of cheap cellos for them. I mean, violin is okay, as far as string instruments go, but to me, nothing comes close to the sound of a cello.

My nights were just as busy as my days. I was practicing my cello three or four hours every night, and there was always homework. I guess if I had to come up with one word to describe my new normal, it would be *crazy-ass busy*. Okay, that's three words, but that's the idea.

Every Saturday, Marcy and I had our lessons with Mr. Majykowski. He'd always pick apart my playing, giving me a long list of things to work on. He never smacked me on the head with a ruler, but it always bugged me that Marcy's list seemed shorter than mine.

"Either I'm better than you," Marcy said, when I started to complain, "or he's cutting me a break because I'm a girl."

"He doesn't seem like the type to cut anyone a break for anything," I grumbled.

"I agree," Marcy said, beaming me a smile. "So that must mean—"

"Oh, shut up."

After our lessons, we'd always spend a few hours working on the boat, usually polishing chrome, cleaning windows, or scrubbing the deck until it was time to go. My audition CD for the Volt competition was due on the first of December. Maybe I was cocky, but I already felt pretty good about my required pieces. I'd been playing the Bach for a couple of years already, thanks to that tough music teacher of mine who'd played cello with the L.A. Philharmonic. I suppose I also had to give some credit to my mom for that: when she read that the L.A. Philharmonic was offering free lessons to promising low-income students of color, she'd signed me up. We didn't have any trouble with the low income or student of color requirements, and at the audition, I ended up playing okay enough to be considered promising.

But the piece that I had to choose myself turned out to be a problem because I just couldn't decide. There were only a few hundred thousand songs to choose from.

Derrick had two suggestions. "Do some jazz," he said. "Or better yet, why not do something way over the top?"

"Like what?"

"What about some hip hop? Why not play something completely wild? Bach is cool, so is jazz, but can you imagine anyone playing some hip hop at a competition like that? One way or the other, you'd stand out."

I laughed. "Yeah, stand out and get run right off the stage. Hip hop? You're crazy!"

Before I got too excited, I decided to run the idea by Mr. Majykowski. I figured he'd veto it straightaway. But at the end of a lesson, when I asked him, he sat there quietly for a few minutes, staring at the wall. "Do it," he sighed. "Hip hop on a cello? I like it. Or jazz, even. Think wild. Who makes up these rules, anyway, that you can only play certain types of music with certain types of musical instruments? You have my blessing. And if any of the judges complain, don't get mad, but . . ."

"Get even?" I finished for him.

"Well, ah, no, I was going to say call me, and I will talk to them. It is my job to be the one who gets mad and even. *Verstehen, du?*

"What?"

"Oh, sorry, I was reading Faust in the original German and my brain is a little stuck on that language. What I asked was, do you understand?"

"Yessir," I said. *What a cool guy.* Who'd have thought it? When I won that $10,000 prize, I'd have to buy him a thank-you present. Or better yet, maybe I'd send him one from California. A basket of avocados, maybe.

At school, Marcy and I would get together at lunch, along with Elvis and some other kids, and then I'd see her again during orchestra. But that was about it. We'd catch up on everything every Saturday morning, talk about this and that and what had happened during the week. But something had changed between us after that bus ride, and I wondered if it had something to do with her dad. When I asked her about it, she just smiled and shook her head. I wondered if she'd somehow sensed that I was planning to take off if something crazy happened and I actually won some money. Maybe that was it.

On the night just before I had to put the audition CD in the mail, Derrick picked me up at Bernice's. We grabbed burgers and fries at Kidd Valley on the way to his office, which was in a run-down business park in South Seattle. He parked and turned on his car alarm, and then we went into the building. We crossed the lobby and then went through another door. And when he flicked on the lights, I thought I'd just stepped onto the starship *Enterprise*. There was a huge computer console and then, through another door, was a room with a microphone stand and stool in the center.

"Here's where the magic happens," Derrick said. "It's all state-of-the-art computers and recording equipment. I spared no expense."

"I can see that."

"Why don't you get set up and warm up. I'll get everything going here. There's an intercom between the rooms. You can also see me through the window. When you're ready to go, just let me know. There's a decent chair for you to use in the closet. Adjust the mike so it's about two inches from your soundboard."

Four hours later, as the last note faded away, I heard Derrick say over the intercom, "That's cool. Let's call it a night."

I was completely spent. My T-shirt was soaked with sweat, and I had a headache. I put away my cello and trudged into the next room. Derrick was leaning back in the chair, sunglasses pushed up on top of his head, looking at me in a way I didn't recognize.

"So what do you think?" I said, slumping down into a chair.

Derrick just stared at me.

"What?"

He shook his head. "I had no idea, bro. You're so damn good. You know, maybe even good enough . . . " And then he shook his head again.

"Maybe what?"

"Ah, it's a crazy idea. We can talk about it some other time. You know, after this is all over. But the sound you can get from your cello, it just knocked me over. I think we've got some great stuff here. I'll dupe it tonight, burn a CD, and you can get it in the mail tomorrow."

"Thanks, Derrick.

"No problem," he said. "Help yourself to a Coke. There's a fridge out front. I'll be just another twenty minutes."

I licked my lips; I was parched. Something cold and liquid sounded good. As I pushed through the door, I could feel Derrick's eyes on me. If I hadn't been so tired, I would have forced him to tell me what he was thinking. It'd just have to wait for some other time.

25

Okay, I'm stubborn. But there was no way I was going to call Mom and see how she was doing. She owed me the first call. She was the adult, and she was the one who'd taken off. And I had been expecting a call for weeks, especially after my episode on the ferry. I figured she'd be worried about her boy and also mad that I'd done something so completely stupid. But instead of a call, she sent me a get-well card. I think she went with that because it was safer. After all, you can't yell at a card or talk back to it. Whatever.

In early November, I did finally get an old-fashioned snail mail letter from her. She may have tried to send me an e-mail, but it'd been weeks since I'd bothered to check. I didn't have my own computer, so I had to do it at school or at the public library. I really didn't have the time.

In her letter, she wrote about her job and the great restaurants in Denver. Leon, her boyfriend, had even taken her to a Broncos game. Mom hated football, so I figured she must really like this guy. She also mentioned that she'd be coming to Seattle for Christmas. No mention about what I might do for the holidays, but I guess I wasn't surprised.

"She planning to bring along her beau?" Bernice asked when I told her about Mom's plans.

"I don't know. She didn't say."

Bernice growled deep in her chest. "Well, I s'pose it would be better if I left it up to you. But she can't stay *here* with that man. You'll need to write her back and tell her that."

"Thanks, Bernice," I said.

"I been thinking about Thanksgiving," Bernice said. "I usually work. I get double time."

"Don't change your plans because of me," I said.

"You don't mind?"

I shrugged. "Mom and I usually celebrated Thanksgiving at Denny's," I said, "or not at all."

"I like Denny's," Bernice nodded. "Why don't we do that? I get off late. Invite your brother."

Before I had a chance to mail a reply to my mom, I got another letter from her. A change of plans, she wrote. Leon had booked a cruise out of Miami for the holidays. Paid for the tickets already, so it was too late to change their plans. Well, that avoided a messy confrontation about Leon. Not that I really gave a rat's ass. I crumpled up her letter and tossed it across the kitchen.

Thanksgiving turned out to be a bust. I had the flu, so it was probably good that we hadn't made any big plans. I didn't eat anything for three days and spent Thanksgiving Day barfing.

On a Tuesday night in mid-December, Derrick brought pizza over for dinner. He said it was a belated Thanksgiving celebration, and Bernice had taken the day off. She said she'd met with an attorney, making sure my staying with her was all legal and correct.

"Like it or not," she'd explained, "you're still a minor in the eyes of the law. And that means that some adult has got to be able to tell the doctors what to do next time you decide to go crazy and jump out of an airplane or something."

"I wouldn't jump out of an airplane," I said. "That would be nuts."

Bernice nodded. "Uh-huh," she said. "That makes me feel much better. I bet a month ago, you'd have said the same thing about jumping off a ferryboat. So pardon me if I don't believe you. Make sure my pizza has anchovies on it, got it?"

I smiled. I'd miss Bernice when I headed back to California. Beneath all the bluster and growling, she was a good person. So there we were, sitting in Bernice's kitchen, eating pizza, drinking root beer, and acting as much like a real family as I could ever remember. The only thing missing was Mom, and I can't say I missed her much. And a dad? What the hell was that?

Bernice was asking questions about Derrick's business. She wanted to know what groups and artists he had under contract, if they were distributing music online, and so on. Derrick knew his stuff, and I could tell Bernice was impressed by his answers. She even asked him if he was interested in taking on investors.

"You thinking about it?" Derrick joked. I couldn't really blame him. I mean, who could have imagined that a black lady bus driver would ever be sophisticated or hip enough or have enough money to be taken seriously about investing in a music company?

Bernice's pizza paused halfway between her mouth and the table. "Get out," she said.

Derrick's mouth dropped open. "Excuse me?" he asked.

"Get out right now, smart ass. You think you can sit there and disrespect me because I'm not rich like Oprah? Pick up your food and git."

I figured the evening was wrecked now and that Derrick wasn't going to let Bernice talk to him that way. I knew what happened to people who disrespected him, and it wasn't pretty. If there'd been someplace to hide, I would have tried to find it. But I was caught between the wall and Derrick, so I did the next best thing.

"Sure, she has money," I said, elbowing Derrick. "So pass the pizza, dipshit, and apologize to your auntie." I closed my eyes and waited for the blow that I knew would be heading my way.

When nothing happened, I opened my eyes to check it out. There was Derrick, just staring at me all big-eyed. And then he started laughing, in that slow way like Eddie Murphy does. I flinched as he reached for me, but he just patted me on the head.

"I'm sorry, Bernice," he said, pushing out of his seat, dropping one knee to the floor and then taking her hand. "You're absolutely right. I'm an asshole. You are, indeed, someone I admire very much. More than you probably know. If you'd like to invest in my business, I'd be more than happy to sit down and go over the numbers and the business plan with you." And then he kissed the back of her hand.

I still thought she was going to punch him out. But she just snatched her hand back and then got a funny, wistful look on her face.

"Sit down," she ordered. "People make mistakes. It's what you do afterwards that counts. I'd probably still be married if I'd learned that earlier in life or if any of my ex-husbands had done what you just did. Apology accepted. Just don't ever talk to me that way again."

"You got it," Derrick said.

I let my breath out in a whoosh. "How'd you learn about all this music and business stuff?" I asked Bernice.

"Don't talk with your mouth full," she replied. "Try again when it's empty."

I rolled my eyes and Derrick laughed, but I did as she asked. I made an exaggerated show of swallowing and then tried again. "So, you know, how did you . . . "

"My second husband was a radio deejay," she said. "I sorta picked up a few things about music from him. Simple as that."

"Can't be that simple," Derrick said.

"Took a few night classes, too," Bernice chuckled. "Business and accounting."

"There you go," Derrick muttered. "That makes more sense."

After the pizza was gone, Bernice grabbed her purple

bowling ball and bright green shoes and left. Derrick and I took our root beers outside and sat down on the front steps. It hadn't rained in a couple of days. It was cool, but not cold. I suppose Derrick might have preferred to drink a real beer or maybe sip some liquor, but he didn't seem to mind. Hard to beat root beer and pizza.

"So what's your plan?" I asked.

"Plan?"

"Yeah, you know, don't get mad, get even and all of that."

"Oh, that plan." Derrick smiled. "Does Bernice have Internet?"

"She doesn't even have a computer," I said.

"Cell phone?"

I shook my head.

Derrick stared at me like I was some creature from the Dark Ages. "Oh, well," he shrugged. "Follow me."

I followed him out to his 1969 Chevrolet Impala, which he'd parked next to the curb. Yeah, *that* was the car that'd followed me on the street that first day after school. It was also the same car I'd noticed after my first time playing downtown. Derrick had been watching out for me since my first few days in Seattle; I guess I was never as alone as I thought.

"I had it zeroed out," Derrick said as I slid into the front seat on the passenger side.

"Meaning what?"

"It means I had this baby rebuilt from the frame up. It's better now than when it came off that Detroit assembly line all those years ago. Smell it?"

He was right. It had that awesome new car smell. Any other day, I'd have been happy to sit there for hours. But now I was more interested in what Derrick had to show me. He pulled a slim laptop from beneath his seat and flipped open the screen.

"Give me a minute. Somebody on this street probably has Wi-Fi. . . . There . . . got it. And not even password protected. That trusting soul deserves to be taught a lesson," he murmured to himself, "but not by me." He winked in my direction, then punched a few keys and tilted the screen so I could see it. "This'll be posted on YouTube tomorrow at 6 a.m., and a link to it will be sent in e-mails to school administrators, Coach Ford, and the newspapers, all from an anonymous e-mail account, by 6:30."

It took me a second to realize what I was watching. "Is that . . . ?"

"Is it ever," Derrick said.

Adrian, Turk, and Bobby were sitting on a bed in what looked like a motel room. The sound was off, but I could tell that they were talking to someone who was standing just out of camera range.

"I thought you were out of that—you know—that kind of business," I said softly. I wasn't sure if Derrick knew that I knew about his time dealing drugs.

Derrick shrugged. "I am," he said, "but I still have ex-business associates. I called in a few favors. Let me turn up the sound. . . . "

"What is it? Coke?" I asked.

Derrick shook his head and smiled. "Not for these white boys. Nope, they're athletes. Or at least they wanna look cut and ripped like the real thing. And you know how it is with dedicated athletes, hoping to get football scholarships from a fine Division II college. They'll do just about anything to make it happen, especially if their daddy's pushing them. Blow isn't their drug of choice. Listen."

As usual, Adrian was doing the talking. The sound quality wasn't great, but it was clear enough. "You sure this is good-quality HGH and not some fake shit from some fertilizer factory in China?" he asked.

"I run a serious business, my man. And sellin' crap don't do nothing to create customer loyalty, you know."

As soon as I heard the voice, I knew who it was. I glanced at Derrick. "You've been busy," I said evenly.

"I couldn't let anyone else have all the fun," Derrick said modestly. "And if you'd known what I was doing, you'd want to get in on it—and that wouldn't have been wise."

Revenge was supposed to feel sweet. But for some strange reason, I just felt empty inside. For weeks, I'd imagined getting even with those three, but now that it was happening, thanks to Derrick, it was a letdown. Nothing was going to bring Ruby back. And short of a personality transplant, I doubted that anything would ever change those jerks.

I watched as Adrian held out his hand, palm up. Bobby glanced at it blankly for a moment and then pulled an envelope from beneath his sweatshirt and handed it over. Adrian passed it to Derrick.

"Aren't you going to count it?" Turk asked, a smirk on his face.

"I know where you live," Derrick replied in a tone that wiped the smirk from Turk's face.

There were a few more seconds of video, and then that was it. "Where'd you get that stuff they bought?" I asked. "HGH? That's human growth hormone, isn't it?"

Derrick nodded. "Yeah, some athletes and old folks take it. It's supposed to help turn you into an incredible hulk. But that's not what I sold them. They bought sugar pills."

"What'll happen to them?"

"Like I said, instead of getting mad, get even. These white boys are about to have their lives turned upside down. I imagine they'll get kicked out of school or at least kicked out of sports. The police are sure to have a chat with them. They'll never know it was me, acting on your behalf, who was responsible. Now, isn't that better than what you had in mind?"

"I suppose so," I admitted. "But it would be nice if they knew it was me."

"No, it wouldn't," Derrick said, faking a slap at my head. "What's with the misguided macho crap? Time to grow up. You know what they say about revenge."

"What's that?"

"It's a taco best served cold."

"Where'd you learn that?" I asked.

Derrick smiled. "I know that Mom thinks I'm just another dumb homeboy, but I didn't waste my time in jail."

"What'd you do?"

"I read books," he said. "Learned a lot from a Japanese dude named Musashi. Check him out sometime."

"I guess I get your point," I said.

"And besides, you gotta figure those three boys, once they get through dealing with this, they'll still be worrying that someone's going to believe your girlfriend. If they're smart, they'll be looking over their shoulder for the next couple of years."

I didn't bother to say Marcy wasn't my girlfriend.

26

On Christmas Eve, after Bernice got off from work, we went out and picked up a cheap tree from a lot that was practically giving them away. We decorated it with twinkle lights and ornaments from a box that Bernice found out in the garage. I didn't tell her that this was the first time I'd ever decorated a Christmas tree, but I think she could tell. She turned out the lights, and it seemed almost magical, glowing there in the corner of the room.

I sniffed the air. The scent of that miserable-looking fir tree filled the room, and I smiled. Now it seemed like Christmas.

Marcy and Elvis joined us in the afternoon on Christmas Day. They didn't seem to mind cold pizza, and Bernice didn't seem to mind that Marcy and I sat together on the couch. Marcy didn't seem to mind my arm around her shoulder, either. We watched a football game, and then Bernice took over the TV, insisting that we watch her favorite holiday movie, *White Christmas*.

"What's a black woman doing with a favorite movie called *White Christmas*?" Elvis asked, with a laugh.

"Don't mess with me," Bernice said, baring teeth as she smiled.

White Christmas was one of those goofy old movies from back when blacks weren't seen much on TV. But after making stupid comments under our breath for the first ten minutes and getting the evil eye from Bernice every time, we finally started paying attention and had to admit that it was kind of good. The actors weren't any I'd heard of, but Bernice knew their names and made sure that by the end of the movie, we did, too. I didn't much like Bing Crosby, but Danny Kaye and Rosemary Clooney were great. When it was over, Bernice made us promise we'd watch it again with her next year. I nodded along with Marcy and Elvis, even though I was going to be long gone by next year. I caught Marcy watching me. I had a feeling she was wondering where I'd be, too.

I spent the rest of the school vacation practicing. I still wasn't sure if I'd be accepted for the semifinals of the competition. To tell the truth, if it wasn't for the prize money, I'd have bagged it right then and there. The Volt competition drew applicants from across the entire United States; only eighteen semifinalists were chosen, and only four would make the finals. Who was I to think that I was one of the best young African-American or Latino cellists in the country? There had to be thousands of kids better than me—kids with two parents at home, whose families had stayed put; kids whose parents could afford the best music teachers money could buy; and kids who spent summers at music camp in Vermont or Vail, while I'd spent summers playing for change on the streets of L.A. and Orange County. Who was I kidding?

The semifinalists were going to be posted on the Volt website at 7 a.m., Eastern Standard Time, on January 2. Derrick said he'd come by and let me use his laptop to check. I didn't think he'd remember, but at 3:45 a.m. on January 2, he was pounding on my bedroom door. I guess Bernice was up, too, and let him in.

"Come on, you lazy slug. Get up! I got coffee in the Impala, the heater's running, and the Wi-Fi from your neighbors is up—so we're good to go." He didn't wait around for a reply.

I threw on some clothes and a sweatshirt, trotted outside, pulled open the car door, and found Bernice sitting in the front passenger seat, all huddled up in this big pink poofy thing with a hood. She was sipping coffee, and she looked up. "I already called shotgun," she said, then pulled the door shut. I was too tired to argue and jumped into the backseat. Derrick handed me a cup of Starbucks, and we all sat there, waiting for 4 a.m. Pacific Standard Time— 7 a.m. back east.

Nobody wanted to talk; it was way too early. I held my cup with two hands, wondering what I was going to do when I didn't see my name on the list. I didn't have a plan B. If I didn't win, I had no idea what I was going to do. The Impala's engine rumbled in the background like a distant bass drum. The heater was pouring out warm air, and I yawned. It'd be easy to fall asleep.

"Here we go, sports fans," Derrick said.

Apparently, that was the signal for Bernice to leave. She pushed open her door, letting the cool morning air rush into the car.

"What are you doing?" I grumbled. "You aren't going to wait?"

"I'm going back to bed," she said. "And by the way, congratulations, Jace." She flashed one of her rare smiles at me and then trundled off across the grass.

Derrick turned around and lifted up his laptop so I could see the screen. There it was, first name on the list: Jace Adams, Seattle, Washington.

"Way to go, bro," Derrick said, slapping me on the shoulder. "Competition's in six weeks. Now what?"

"Practice," I said. I couldn't hide the grin. "That's what everybody else'll be doing, so I just need to make sure I practice more than the rest of them—and harder." *And at least for a few weeks, I don't need to worry about a plan B.*

"Sounds like you got it covered. You hungry?"

"Always."

"Come on, then. My treat."

27

The next few weeks raced by. January was unseasonably warm in Seattle. The skiers complained, but I didn't mind. One evening each week, I played downtown. I didn't tell Marcy or Mr. Majykowski. They would have thought it was a waste of time, if not downright dangerous, but I needed the money.

Besides, I knew it wasn't dangerous. Sir Lionel was always at the end of the block, watching over me like some dirty, crazy guardian angel. And at least once each night, I'd hear a familiar rumble and see Derrick's Impala cruise by. I wasn't worried about any local gang deciding to take an interest in me. Derrick had made sure to get the word out. You see a black kid playing cello, leave him alone. Word had also gotten out about what had happened to Adrian, Bobby, and Turk. I suppose it didn't take a computer genius to put two and two together and suspect that it had been some sort of retribution for what had happened to me.

I'd even heard Elvis hint that he'd been involved in getting back at them for what they'd done to him that first month of school, as well as what they'd done to his friend—me. I almost said something about it to him, but I guess I didn't really mind. If anyone was going to take credit for it, I was glad it was Elvis. And if it kept others from getting in his face, even better.

I just knew that those three would never show their faces around school again. The day after the video had appeared on YouTube, the local newspaper and TV stations had run stories about it. All three had been expelled from school, and the local prosecutor had even considered filing charges against them, though nothing had happened—yet. The first day back at school after the holidays, I'd heard some guys in the hallway saying that Bobby's and Turk's parents had sent them off to some sort of wilderness survival boys camp in Bumf*&k, Utah. And Adrian had been sent to live with grandparents back east somewhere. Like I said, I didn't care what happened to them. I just hoped they wouldn't hurt anyone else. Derrick told me it wasn't my worry anymore, but I worried anyway. How do you convince someone who likes hurting people to stop? Had Derrick's little trick taught them a lesson? I had my doubts.

I didn't even wonder how Mom might be doing. I knew if things were going okay, I wouldn't hear a thing, but if she and lover boy were on the outs, I'd find her sitting on Bernice's porch some evening playacting like life was all just ice cream and cake.

Every Saturday, Mr. Majykowski would listen to me play, nodding silently, his eyes closed, and then when I was finished, we'd go over it again. He'd pick on each note, each pause, the way my hands and bow worked, the length of each note. He never yelled. He never called me stupid. But he didn't allow any mistake to sneak by. He was as relentless as some kind of mythical creature that never stops, never compromises, never stops hunting for its prey.

In my case, his prey was imperfection. I suppose this is where I'm just like him. I wanted it perfect, too. I figured that if I played it perfectly, the judges would have no other choice. They couldn't pick that kid from New York City who'd spent all his life going to the best music schools money could buy. They'd have to pick the loser from California.

The competition was scheduled for Sunday, February 15. It was going to begin at nine in the morning in the performing arts center on the campus of the University of Washington. All the semifinalists would play in the morning. The judges would pick the four finalists over lunch. We'd have the afternoon to practice, and then the finals would be that night.

The day before the contest, Marcy called and told me she was sick. She was going to have to skip Mr. Majykowski's lessons. I knew she was lying, and I think she knew that I knew. But I just said okay. She was giving up her time with Mr. Majykowski for me. I owed her—a lot.

I rode over to Bainbridge Island on the upper deck of the ferry, standing with my feet braced wide apart up at the front, exposed to the full brunt of the icy blast. The sky was filled with evil-looking clouds boiling in from the west. The water was streaked with foam, as if some giant prehistoric bird was raking the surface with his talons. I had to admit, I was going to miss all of this when I moved back to California.

When I got to Majykowski's yacht, he invited me to eat first, which was unusual. Except for our first visit, he'd never offered food. He served tomato soup and cheese sandwiches. After I finished my sandwich and soup, we went into Mr. Majykowski's sitting room. I tuned up my cello, played a couple of warm-up exercises, and then I was ready to go.

"Play your program just like you're going to do it tomorrow," Mr. Majykowski said. "When you're all done, we'll talk about it. Good, ya?"

I took a deep breath and then began. A strange thing happens when I play music. Time begins to go wacky. I'm not sure why, but as I played the notes, I went somewhere else. I guess it was one of those sci-fi kind of things.

I finished my required pieces and then began the last one. Derrick had wanted me to play some hip hop, and I'd been tempted. I'd even gotten Mr. Majykowski's okay. Marcy and Elvis had suggested something more pop. But in the end, I had decided to play something that Sir Lionel had suggested, an old jazz classic called "Take Five." When I played the last note, it seemed to echo on as if it didn't want to die. I was motionless, bow ready to play another note, afraid that if I moved a muscle, it would break the spell.

Mr. Majykowski began to clap, the sound of his mutilated hands slapping together startling me. I relaxed in my chair and looked up at him, ready for the criticisms to begin, but he just kept clapping, his craggy, bearded face warmed with a smile.

"Bravo," he said, finally.

"And?"

"No *and*," he said, his voice thick with emotion. "Bravo. It is the only word that is appropriate for what I have just heard. Your playing was extraordinary. Whether you win this competition tomorrow or not, you have just showed me what you are made of, Mr. Jace Adams. You are one of the chosen few. The sky is the limit for you, my young friend. You have a remarkable, remarkable musical gift. You don't just play the music, you breathe it, you become part of it, you live it, and by doing so, you reach out and change anyone listening."

I didn't know what to say after all that. I knew I'd played just about as well as I could, but I also knew that that hadn't stopped Mr. Majykowski from picking my playing apart in the past.

"So where do you want me to start?"

"Start?"

"Yeah, you know, what could I have done better?"

"Did you not hear what I said, Jace?"

I rolled my eyes. "Yeah, whatever. But this is my last lesson before the competition."

"I know, and you have done me proud with all of your hard work and dedication—and playing once a week on the street. . . . "

I began to protest, but he held up his hand to stop me.

"You think Sir Lionel was not my eyes and ears? He kept an eye on you for himself and for you—but also for me. Now, go home. Call up your friend Marcy, and go out and have some pizza or something. Get a good night's sleep. I see you tomorrow."

"That's it?" I asked.

"It? No, my friend. This is just the beginning for you. Mark my words."

He helped me into my jacket, stuffed a bag full of chocolate chip cookies into the front pocket, and then patted me awkwardly on the shoulder. "Godspeed, Jace Adams," he said as I stepped off his boat, carrying my green cello case.

I'd swear there were tears in his eyes as I left. I figured it must have been the wind.

28

When I woke the next morning, there were new clothes hanging on my door. Black suit, white shirt, black tie. New black shoes and black socks. I even had new boxer shorts. *Damn.* I showered and dressed in my new clothes. And strange as it may sound, I wasn't feeling nervous. Who was I kidding? I knew I didn't have a chance.

"Thanks for the, well, everything," I said to Bernice. I was sipping coffee and eating a banana, being careful not to stain my new shirt.

"No problem," Bernice said. "I didn't think you and your lunatic teacher would have thought about it. I called up your girlfriend and Elvis. We made a day of it. Decided to go for the Obama look. And if you don't like it, you can blame Marcy. It was her idea."

I admired myself in the window reflection: I didn't look half bad.

I heard a rumble outside. Derrick had arrived. "If I make the finals, you'll come, right?" I asked, gulping the last bit of coffee.

"Wouldn't miss it, honey."

They kept all of us in a room backstage while each person played. We couldn't hear anyone else's performance. And nobody backstage wanted to talk. I tried one kid, and he looked at me like I was a piece of unwanted puke, so I didn't try again. As I sat there, I didn't think about the music. I thought, instead, about my mom. I was wondering what she was doing. I even hoped she was all right. I guess that just goes to show you what a loser I am. She runs off without even saying anything, and I'm not even tough enough to stay mad at her. I'd thought about sending her a note and inviting her to the contest. But I didn't. Why bother?

A stern-looking woman finally came into the room and tapped me on the shoulder. "You're next," she said. "Good luck."

She led me into a warm-up room and closed the door without saying anything. I pulled my cello out of the case, extended the spike, and then ran through a few exercises and scales. I still wasn't nervous. I didn't expect to make the finals, so what was there to be nervous about?

There was a knock on the door, and I heard a voice say, "We're ready for you, Mr. Adams." That was cool: Mr. Adams.

I was grinning like an idiot as I walked out onto the stage, which was bright with light. The hall beyond was in the dark. I could barely make out a table with six people— the judges—sitting behind it. The hall was deserted except for them. I guess they didn't want any cheerleaders unduly influencing their decisions. I hadn't thought of that, and I wondered where Derrick, Elvis, Marcy, and the rest of them had ended up.

"Whenever you're ready, Mr. Adams," said a disembodied voice from a speaker in the shadows above.

I took my seat, plucked the strings, adjusted the pegs, and then began.

It was all over before I realized it, the sound of my last note fading to nothing. I blinked my eyes and looked up. No applause, no nothing. I could have been playing on a sidewalk to a deserted street.

"Thank you, Mr. Adams. We'll post the results in an hour."

And that was that. I had no idea how I'd done. Honest. I couldn't remember a thing.

I found my case in the back room, put away my cello, and then walked over to the student union building. Marcy, Bernice, Professor Majykowski, Derrick, and Elvis were all crowded around a table, trying not to look nervous. They jumped up as I approached.

"What are you doing here, Bernice?" I said. She was dressed in her bus driver uniform.

"I couldn't stay away," she said, smiling.

"So tell us," Elvis said. "You were brilliant, right?"

Marcy pushed a cup of coffee in my direction. I took a sip and shrugged. "I have no idea. I don't remember any of it."

"You don't remember?" Derrick said. He pushed his sunglasses up onto his forehead.

I shrugged again. "I started, and then I was playing the last note. I have no memory of what happened in between."

Majykowski smiled and nodded. "That is a very good sign. You were in the—how you say it?"

"Zone." Bernice suggested as she reached out and squeezed my arm.

"Yes, the zone," he said, his accent thickening as he became excited. "The music zone. I am sure you were brilliant."

An hour later, I trudged back to the performance hall, everyone tagging along behind me. Marcy hadn't said much while we waited. I'd catch her watching me from time to time, but when I looked at her, she'd look away.

Some guy from the Volt competition was standing in the foyer, surrounded by performers and friends and the curious. He was middle-aged, wearing a gray suit, and had the hunched look of somebody who spent his days trapped behind a desk. He straightened his red tie and then began by thanking everyone for coming and praising all of the semifinalists. And then he started reading the names.

I didn't bother to pay attention. He wasn't going to say my name. I was rehearsing how I would apologize to everyone for being such a screw-up. I'd need to say how sorry I was to Majykowski first thing. And Derrick, too. I wasn't sure what I'd say to Elvis, Marcy, and Bernice.

And then they were all pounding me on the back, and Marcy and Elvis were hugging me.

"There was no doubt," Professor Majykowski announced, his face beaming. "As soon as you said you were in the zone, I knew you make the finals. I just knew it."

"I'm . . . I'm glad one of us knew," I stuttered. I couldn't believe it. I'd made the finals. This was just insane. And for the first time, the idea of winning seemed like it might be more than wishful thinking. *Maybe I could win after all?*

"We'll clear out," Elvis said, "let you practice and rest. Each of the finalists has been assigned a practice room. I'll find out yours." He put on his "you don't want to mess with me" face and took off.

And for the first time, I suppose, I really truly began to think that maybe, just maybe I could win enough money to leave. Who knows? If things worked out, I might even be surfing within a week. I looked down at my hands: they were shaking. *Now* I was nervous. Now I had something to lose. I should have been elated. But my old friend, fear, was back.

I spent the afternoon practicing, working on little snippets of the compositions I'd be playing that evening before the judges and a packed audience. When I wandered out of my room, I avoided the other contestants, keeping to myself. I took a break at about 4 p.m. I needed some food. They had fruit and cookies set out for everyone, but I wanted something else, so I walked over to the student union building and bought a toasted cheese sandwich and a drink.

I was almost back when I heard a shout. "Yo, Prince of Seattle." Sir Lionel stepped out from behind a tree and onto the sidewalk up ahead.

"What are you doing so far from home, Sir Lionel?" I was happy to see him.

"You, my boy. You are being tested for knighthood. I came to prevent the prince of darkness from disrupting your quest."

I glanced around, wondering if that was his way of saying I was about to be jumped. "No problem," I said nervously. "I'm glad you're here. Will you come inside and listen?"

"Oh, no, I couldn't. My place is out here. I will prevent the prince from entering, with my life, if I must."

"Hopefully, it won't come to that," I remarked. I thought about shaking his hand, but I knew he didn't like people to touch him. That's why I was surprised when he suddenly grabbed me and gave me a hug.

"Be brave," he whispered in my ear, "and go with the blessings of the master of the universe. I have already foreseen your destiny."

"Do I win?" I asked.

"You will not fail," Sir Lionel replied. With that, he released me from his grasp and returned to his guard post under the tree.

Just four of us were playing now. They'd randomly selected the order, and I was going last. I'd wait in my room until it was my turn. After we'd all played, the judges would vote, then line us up onstage to announce the winners.

When the wait was over, someone knocked on my door, like earlier in the day. I grabbed my cello and bow and followed the person out onto the stage. In the darkness beyond the stage, I felt more than saw the people crowding the seats and balcony. My friends were out there somewhere, and outside under the tree, Sir Lionel was at his post. But it didn't make me feel any better.

I took my seat and began to play. And as it had earlier in the day, time seemed to disappear. But unlike what happened in the morning, this time I was aware of every note and hesitation, of each bit that goes into playing music. And as if that wasn't enough, I also thought about my mother and what she'd done to me and about the father I'd never known. I thought about my friends and about floating in the water with Ruby. It was sort of like that now, with the notes holding me up instead of Ruby. I knew they'd always been there, keeping my head above the water, so I poured everything I had into them until I totally merged with them.

There was a pause when I finished the last piece. But this time, instead of hearing the dry voice of one of the judges, I heard the audience exploding with applause. I heard someone in the back yelling, "Bravo, bravo," and I knew it was Professor Majykowski.

I stood and blinked into the bright lights, then snapped out of my stupor and, remembering what Marcy'd told me to do, bowed. Then I left the stage, and someone gave me a bottle of water. I was joined by the three other finalists, and we were led back on onstage.

A man in a wheelchair rolled onto the stage, winking at me as he passed; it was Mr. Blue, who wheeled up to the microphone and began to speak. He thanked everyone for coming, then said that as the major underwriter for the Volt, he was thrilled by the quality of the finalists; to him, we were all winners.

"What a crock of shit," whispered the kid standing next to me. "Get on with it you old—"

"Cut the crap," I warned under my breath, before he could finish.

He sneered in my direction, but I noticed he moved slightly away from me and kept his mouth shut. I guess he'd gotten my point. Smart kid.

Then Mr. Blue began announcing the winners: "Fourth place tonight goes to Rachel Sanchez of Santa Fe, New Mexico."

There was polite applause from the audience as a girl at the end of the line walked up to Mr. Blue and shook his hand. He handed her a plaque, and then she took a quick bow and rushed off the stage. I could see tears in her eyes.

"Third place . . . Dexter Fisher."

Now that snotty kid I'd threatened pasted a phony smile on his face and went over to Mr. Blue. They shook hands politely. The boy accepted his plaque and an envelope, took his bow, and then walked off the stage, eyeing me coldly as he passed.

"I want to commend our remaining performers," Mr. Blue said. "Each is an exceptional musician."

The girl I was standing next to was about my height, and she smiled nervously at me. "If they don't hurry up," she whispered, "I'm going to pee in my pants." I had to choke back a laugh; she was my kind of girl.

And then it hit me: there were only two of us left. And that's when this weird time thing started to happen. Everything slowed down, and all the colors seemed to get brighter; the sound of the audience changed from excited noise and babbling to a kind of music. I could see Bernice and Derrick, plus Marcy and Elvis in the audience, big grins on all their faces. And then I spotted Professor Majykowski and his wife. They were all looking at me with such pride and even love, I thought I was going to faint; it was almost too much to take.

I'd gone from such a long time of feeling like nobody

really cared much about me, let alone actually *liked* me, to having real friends and—Bernice—and even reconnecting with my brother. In the space of a couple of months, I'd somehow found this weird and awesome collection of people—and they were all like family to me.

"Second place: Jace Adams."

There was a whoop from the crowd, and I felt my heart flutter just a beat. "Congratulations," I said to the girl.

"Thanks," she said. "I don't know what I would have done if I'd lost. This was my last try."

I walked up to Mr. Blue in a daze and shook his hand. "You were marvelous, Jace," he said. "I hope you'll come back and try again next year." He squeezed my hand hard.

"Thank you, sir," I said. And that's when something clicked; I felt a rush of warmth go through my body. And as I looked out at the faces I'd grown to love, I realized that even though I'd lost, nothing had changed. They were still smiling and yelling for me just as if I'd won. I may not have taken first place, but I wasn't any kind of loser—not anymore.

29

"You should have won," Marcy snapped. "Everyone heard it—no one could touch you."

I couldn't explain it to her, so I just shrugged. "It's all right," I said. "It is what it is. . . . "

"No it isn't," Marcy snapped. "We should get Elvis's father involved. This is *sooo* not fair!"

"It's okay, Marcy," I said. "Seriously." Maybe my brain was turning to sludge, but I even meant what I said. I mean, like, second place was even better than a dream come true for me—because deep down, I'd never figured I was good enough to ever get this far.

Bernice'd invited everyone over to her house for a celebration after the recital, and while they were all inside, Marcy and I sat on the front steps. Through the windows, I could hear Professor Majykowski talking about the recital, his voice so loud that it was rattling the glass. And then even Sir Lionel showed up; somebody with a pickup truck had given him a ride, with his cart stowed in the back.

"I lost, Sir Lionel," I said, as he pushed his cart up to the front door.

Sir Lionel looked at me with surprise, glanced into the house, and then smiled at me. "No—you didn't," he said. "Food?"

"Inside," I said. He patted me on the shoulder as he stepped past us and went inside. I guess that was when I finally realized he was right.

When we were alone again, Marcy said, "So when are you leaving?"

"Leaving?"

"Don't go there," she said. "Just don't. I've known all along that you were counting on that money to, you know. And second place was worth what, $5,000?"

"How did you know I was thinking about—"

"Leaving?" Marcy finished it for me, pushing her hair out of her eyes. "Turns out you get kinda talkative when you just about kill yourself. And that stuff the doctors shot you up with probably didn't hurt."

"So you knew?"

"It wasn't like it was hard to guess," she said, with a shrug. "And it must make it easier, knowing Derrick's been asked to move back to California for his job."

"What are you talking about, Marcy?"

Marcy covered her mouth and looked horrified. "Oh, crap. He's going to kill me. I was sure you knew!"

I shook my head, but it made sense, and I was happy for him. If they wanted him moving back there, he must be getting a promotion.

"That's cool for him," I said. "He probably didn't say anything because he didn't want me to worry before the competition."

Marcy nodded hopefully.

"Well, I'm sorry to disappoint you and Elvis," I said. "Up until Mr. Blue handed me my check, I knew what I was going to have to do. But then, when I actually had it in my hands, it all changed. I—"

"I hate you, Jace Adams!" Marcy interrupted. Her head was down, so I couldn't see her face. "I thought I'd be okay with this, but I'm not. You know, you just can't keep running every time life doesn't go your way—"

"I'm sticking around," I said.

"And I'm just so sick of you being so selfish and—" Marcy looked up at me. I could see she was all upset; she looked teary.

"Seriously?" she said. "Because if you're just saying that, I'll—"

"Seriously," I said. "I promise you. I changed my mind, and I'm going to stay—for now."

"Get outta here," Marcy shrieked and then punched my shoulder.

"What'd you do that for?" I said.

Marcy smiled and punched me again. "Because you deserve it. You were probably gonna stay all along. You're just getting back at me for being so bitchy that first day in orchestra. So now you got your revenge. Happy?"

She turned away from me, but she was still smiling. We sat there in silence for a while. Then she said, "So what'll you do with all that money?"

I was completely confused; I thought she'd be happy I was sticking around, but she still seemed pissed in some way. "I guess I'd hide most of it in the leg of my bed," I said, with a crooked grin.

Marcy elbowed me in the ribs, but then squeezed my arm tightly. "Most of it? What about the rest?"

"Uh, well, I'm going to use it to buy some surfboards and some wet suits," I said.

"*Surfboards*, as in more than one?" she asked.

I nodded.

Marcy laughed. "So you really *do* surf?"

I nodded again. "Yeah, I really do."

"You know, Elvis and I always figured that you were just making up the surfing thing. But we didn't say anything. We didn't want to hurt your feelings."

"Now I *am* hurt," I said in mock outrage. "Not only can I surf, but I have plans to do a little teaching so I don't have to surf alone. Can you swim?"

"Yeah," Marcy replied warily.

"Great, then it's a date."

"Date? You mean, as in a *date* date?"

"The Goldbergs are off to the Oregon coast this summer. They invited me and Bernice to come stay with them, and Elvis said I could bring a friend if I wanted. And I think he knew who that'd be."

"Omigod! On vacation with *two* guys? Even with all the parents around, my dad'll never let me go," Marcy shook her head, her eyes sad with regret.

"Nah, it's a done deal. I already talked to him," I said. "And you may remember, he's the one who thinks I'm an awesome cellist and can do no wrong, no matter what color I am."

"No way!" Marcy shrieked.

"Way," I insisted. "I figure Elvis is a lost cause. That hair'll make balancing on the board a nightmare. But he's stubborn, so who knows? He'll probably try it anyway. You, on the other hand, have the makings of a perfectly right-eous surfer babe."

"Did you just call me a *babe*?" Marcy snapped, pre-tending to be indignant.

"I guess I did," I said. "That okay with you?" I put my arm around her waist and pulled her closer.

Marcy thought for a moment. "Probably not," she said, leaning into my side. "But if I'm a babe, what does that make you? Surfer Stringz just doesn't sound quite right."

"How about *Bob*," I said, "as in Surfer Bob?"

"Babe and Bob," Marcy said softly. "That's incredibly lame, you know. And besides, no self-respecting black guy would ever pick the name *Bob*."

"Um, are you forgetting *Bob* Marley?" I said, wagging a finger in the air. "Black! A musician and a Bob. And I bet you didn't know that before he got into reggae, he was training to be a classical cellist."

She gave me a blank stare, then said, "So you're really staying?"

"There's no place like home," I said quietly.

"*Wizard of Oz?*" Marcy said.

"More like *The Wiz*," I said.

And then I did what I'd been wanting to do since that first time on the ferry: I kissed her.

Acknowledgments

Thanks to Peter for appreciating words and music as much as I do, and to Evelyn for her keen editorial eye, timely advice, and for suggesting the idea for this story in the first place.